The Hidden Secret of Towering Pines Manor

The Young Detectives' Mystery
Book Three
by

G.L. Schulze

Published by GLS Press

Book design copyright @ Holli Chlebowski

Cover design by Holli Chlebowski – Graphic Designer

Cover photograph by G. L. Schulze

Published in the United States of America

ISBN: 13:978-0692364642

ISBN: 10:0692364641

Juvenile Fiction/ General/Action Adventure

Other Books by G. L. Schulze

The Young Detectives' Mystery Series:

The Secret Treasure of Pirate's Cove – Book One
The Top Secret Secret of Teddy Rigetta – Book Two

Dedication

For everyone who believes in the paranormal.

Chapter One

It was only four days since they had rescued Teddy and Mai Su. And in that time the world had continued without them. The final plans for the Halloween festivities had been made and their coveted positions of Dracula and the Mummy were assigned to someone else. They were disappointed when they heard the news, but they both knew that rescuing Teddy and Mai Su held a far greater value than scaring the wits out of everyone.

The second thing was that Willie and Kurt discovered they were no longer the new kids in town. Someone had moved into the vacant house at the end of town called Towering Pines Manor. They were ecstatic. That meant no more stares, no more pointing fingers and no more hushed whispers behind cupped hands. They couldn't wait to get back to school and find out who the next *new kid* was.

That Monday morning, Kurt was still pumped from the weekend. He was anxious to relive the events one more time with Willie on the way to school. So anxious that he was waiting on his front porch steps when Willie came by so they could walk together, an everyday occurrence since they met and fought a year ago. They talked and laughed about their exciting weekend even though they had gone over it at least ten times already. Here and there, along the sidewalk a student would join them, falling in behind, listening intently and asking questions, excited and enthralled by their adventure. By the time they reached Danton Rivers High School West, they were completely surrounded by inquisitive boys and girls, most who never, until today, had even said hello to them.

As students crowded around them, both boys leaned brazenly against the stair rail. They were happy in their new notoriety as they told their story of the rescue one more time. They were heroes of course, especially when Teddy arrived at the school on crutches accompanied by a glowing Mai Su McKnight. And of course, the four of them had to tell their story one more time. It wasn't until the black Chrysler Limited Edition 310 drove up that the attention of the crowd was finally diverted.

The car crept around the corner amidst the jabbering excitement of the crowd and pulled up to the curb, its only tell-tale approach was the crunch of dried leaves beneath the wheels. Smooth and sleek like a clipper ship skimming waves, the black Chrysler commanded attention. One by one, the students turned to stare at the car, its dark- tinted windows obscured any occupants. Everyone focused in silence as the driver emerged from behind the wheel. He stepped out smartly, oblivious to the hush that enveloped the school yard. Quickly he adjusted his hat and tie and went around to the back door. It opened noiselessly. A pair of black leather boots, followed by one of the most beautiful girls ever to attend Danton Rivers High School stepped out.

She was tall and slim. As she straightened on the sidewalk, she tossed her head from side to side, her hair dancing in the wind like rippling waves on an ocean, before falling in a lustrous sheen about her shoulders. She tugged down the dark min- skirt and adjusted the beret that now perched precariously on the right side of her head. The silence finally caught her attention and she looked about at the gawking faces that filled the school yard. She sighed, rolled her eyes, slid her sunglasses on and reached for the leather book satchel her driver handed her.

"Be here exactly at three- thirty, Richard."

"Yes, Miss Demming."

His breath caught in his throat. His heart hammered in his chest. It was becoming more difficult to breathe. His eyes prickled with the unblinking dryness of an absolute stare. In that moment Willie knew he was in love. He watched, mesmerized, when she tossed her head back, the long auburn tresses caught the wind lighting the copper highlights before she adjusted the beret to her head. He watched as she clutched the satchel and walked through the parting crowd of silent gawkers, up the stairs right in front of Kurt and him and he blurted out with a guttural croak, "Hi!" For some stupid reason, it seemed the only word he was able to remember.

She stopped and with slow deliberation, she turned her head slightly and pulled her sunglasses down to peer at him over the rims. "Have I spoken to you at all?" Her tone was smooth and crystal and cold as ice.

"Well...ah..no," Willie mumbled and the pink of embarrassment rose on his face.

"Then let's leave it that way." She turned and entered the school. Stunned, no one said a word.

"Wow!" Kurt finally exclaimed, letting out his breath. "What was all that about?"

"I don't know. Who cares! She spoke to me!" Shocked, Kurt turned to stare at his friend. He'd never known Willie to be stupefied by a girl before.

"She was rude if you ask me..." Kurt began, but was cut off by another student.

"She's a snob. A rude snob," Tyler Franklin spat out. A pudgy tenth grader with green streaked blond hair and a face peppered with freckles, he stuck his tongue at the new girl's retreating back. "You should have seen her when she came to town to do some shopping yesterday. She was rude to everyone. Stuck her nose up in their air like she was better than anyone else around here."

"Yeah, she thinks she's so cool with that stupid driver and black car! Big deal!" Clint Kerby agreed. Clint was a running back for the high school football team. He was tall and muscular with shocks of blond hair that brushed his shoulders and bright green eyes that melted the hearts of every girl at Danton Rivers High. He was a straight A student and was always more than willing to help tutor anyone that needed help. Generally, Clint Kerby never had anything bad to say about anyone, least of all a girl.

"I wonder why?" Kurt mused.

"Who cares. She's a snob and word got around fast. Nobody likes her. Nobody wants anything to do with her. Just because they live in that fancy house on the hill," Jessica Carr said with a sneer, her best friend, Rose, nodding at her side. And that comment was the strangest of all because Jessica Carr, whose father owned The Footwear, and Rose Tretheway, whose mother owned The Right Cut Beauty Salon, were the two snobbiest girls in Fisherman's Haven.

"Well, there's the bell," Willie shrugged. "We'd better get going."

Madison Demming, the *new* girl, was made to stand in front of every class and give her name and where she was from. By noon she had grown sufficiently irritated so that she sat at a corner table in the lunch room all by herself. But part of that wasn't by her choice. Her snobby reputation had preceded her into every class. The lunch room was no different. All the students passed the table, sniffed the air, stuck their noses up and kept on walking. By the time the three- thirty bell rang and Madison Demming entered the back seat of her Chrysler Limited Edition 310, she was angry, disgusted and hated Fisherman's Haven worse than Kurt ever could have dreamed.

That was the *first* day of school for the new kid. And every day for the rest of the week was the same. Madison Demming was as cold as the November winds that blew in the first snowflakes from the north on that first day of the month. She spoke to no one and only answered in class when she was called upon by the teacher. No one spoke to her. The crowds didn't part for her like they did on that first day. She had to weave around them. It was as though she didn't exist except for the rude comments whispered overly loud in the halls, and the obvious fact that all the students went out of their way to stay out of hers. She walked to classes alone, staring straight ahead , as though oblivious to her surroundings. She sat in class, alone and straight-backed with her nose stuck out at those around her as though there was no one else there. She couldn't wear her sunglasses in class and little by little, day after day, the haughty expression began to droop. Her face seemed to pale more and more as each day passed. Soon the haunted look of sleepless nights began to show in grey patches beneath her puffy eyes.

And then one day, well into the third week of November, when the first smattering of snow covered the ground, the black Chrysler Limited Edition 310 didn't come. Instead, as though to shock everyone at the school that day, Madison Demming was seen walking to school *with* someone. Not just any someone. She was walking and chatting with Zola Dostoevsky, as though they were really good friends. This time not only did Willie's jaw drop, but so did Kurt's.

"Well, what do you make of that?" Kurt blurted out in complete surprise, more to himself than to Willie. He came to a stop on the sidewalk pulling Willie beside him.

"Don't know. Maybe they have something in common," Willie shrugged. Since that first day of ogling at Madison Demming like a love crazed idiot, Willie had kept his thoughts and his bulging eyes to himself. He'd taken a ribbing from Kurt for nearly three days before Kurt finally let up and let it be after Willie threw Zola Dostoevsky in Kurt's face.

"What? What on earth could they possibly have in common? Zola comes from a poor family and has next to nothing and she's as sweet as the day is long. Miss Snob has all the money money can buy. We all know her personality lies with Hecate, the destroyer of life. What could they possibly have in common?" Kurt cried.

"How should I know!" Willie exclaimed. "Want to go ask?"

"Don't be stupid!" Kurt spat out.

"Well, then I guess it's none of our business."

"You're right, William," Olivia Hurst, the ninth grade English teacher said as she walked past them on the sidewalk. "And Hecate? It's nice to see you actually pay attention in class, Kurt."

Both boys reddened. "Sorry," Kurt mumbled.

"Come on. The bell is going to ring any second now," Willie said. They slowed their steps just enough to allow Miss Hurst to get ahead of them. They watched the two girls for just a moment more while they said their goodbyes. Then Zola turned towards the grade school and Madison to the high school. A strange match. A strange match indeed.

Chapter Two

She lay in her bed tossing and turning, caught between sleep and wakefulness. Somewhere the distant whimper of a baby shushed by the soothing humming of a lullaby penetrated her subconscious and she struggled to climb out of the darkness. There were strange shadows moving and twitching along the wall, a thin gyrating slip of a darkness that swayed first one way then the next. Her heart raced, thudding against her chest and the fear that gripped her froze her to the bed. She struggled against the unseen terror and her eyes flew open. They were still blurry and she wasn't sure where she was. The room was in a state of semi-darkness and here and there were blinding flashes of light tearing through. She stared about her in horror, her eyes drawn to the gyrating shadow. She cowered beneath the quilts and sucked in her breath. She pressed herself back into the mattress wishing and praying she could just completely hide inside it.

She pressed her eyes shut willing the shadow to go away. The eerie empty silence of the room magnified into such deep stillness she felt she was suffocating. She forced herself to open her eyes and confront the danger. They flew open, fixating on the swirling shadow in front of her. She held her breath and with one explosive blast of air from her lungs, Madison Demming sat bolt upright in bed and swore at herself.

"Damn! It's only the shadow of that stupid tree!" She flung the covers and jumped out of the bed, flipping the bedside lamp on. "Should have made sure this stupid drape was closed all the way before I came to bed." She reached for the cord but the darkness outside caught her attention. She stared at the back yard. There was an eerie glow where the snow-covered ground was illuminated in a dim light that switched to dark when the clouds swept across the sliver of a moon. Her breath caught in her throat when a movement leapt from the shadow of the house. She sighed with relief when a deer stopped to look hesitantly behind itself, then bolted into the forest. She jerked on the drapery cord.

A scream pierced the darkness behind her. She whirled around, the cord clenched in her white knuckled hands. Fear once more gripped her and she pressed against the wall unable to move. Her heart jumped to her throat and she couldn't breathe until the second scream shattered her fear.

"*Mom*!" she shouted and raced from the room.

Her mom's room was only two doors away and it was a matter of seconds before she flung her mom's door open and ran inside. She fumbled for the switch on the bedside lamp, mumbling when she couldn't find it. Her fingers were shaking and tears welled in her eyes. Suddenly the overhead lights came on and Madison was pushed aside by Marilyn Winthrop, the live in nurse hired by her father. She was tugging the sleeve of her bathrobe on as she approached the bed.

"Mrs. Demming! Mrs. Demming!" The nurse called out in an authoritative but calm voice. She tried to grab hold of Mrs. Demming, who was on the bed hysterical, jumping from spot to spot across the mattress as if it were on fire while screaming and pointing around the room.

"He's there! I saw him! He's there! He's coming for me! He's going to kill me!"

"Mom! Stop! You'll hurt yourself!" Madison cried running from one side of the bed to the other to prevent her mother from flinging herself off. Her mother's face was white, her eyes bulging with an unknown terror as they darted around the room. Saliva was running down her mouth as she screamed. She didn't notice Madison at all.

"Hush girl! You'll only spread the panic more!" Nurse Winthrop cried over her shoulder.

"Mrs. Demming!" Nurse Winthrop finally scrambled up onto the bed and was able to wrap her arms around the frantic woman. She hugged her tight, edging slowly towards the end of the bed, finally kneeling and bringing Mrs. Demming down with her. By this time, Mrs. Demming had slipped into a numbing silence and allowed herself to be assisted. The nurse stepped down from the bed and with Madison's help, managed to get Mrs. Demming to lie down. "Come now. It's all right. It was just a dream. Just a dream. There, there, now let's just lie down here. That's a good girl. I have your medication."

"Please don't give her that. You'll get her addicted!" Madison was crying. She smoothed the damp hair from her mother's face and groaned inside at the pitiful whimpering noises coming from her mother. She reached for the tissue box that had been knocked on the floor and gently wiped the saliva from her mom's face.

"Stop that. Don't you see your mother has had another episode? This is the only thing that can calm her. Now step out of my way." Nurse Winthrop took out a syringe and injected it into Mrs. Demming's arm. "There. In a few minutes she'll be all right. You'd best be off to your own bed," she ordered Madison .

"No! I'm staying!" Madison declared.

"I think…"

"I don't care what you think!" Madison angrily wiped the tears from her face and stared with defiance at Nurse Winthrop. Since they'd come here, come to this horrible house with its noises and moanings and nightmares, Madison had tried to be brave, but day after day she could feel her mother slipping away. Day after day she could feel Nurse Winthrop taking control, twisting her mother from her until she'd felt so alone, so scared. But tonight she was determined not to be pushed aside. She was determined to stand her ground.

"She's my mother and I'm staying. I'll stay long enough for her to fall asleep. Then I'll go. I just want to be sure she's going to be all right."

"Well," Nurse Winthrop hesitated. "I guess that would be all right. Not long though." She went to the door and gave Mrs. Demming and Madison a long, searching look before closing the door behind her.

Madison waited until the door closed. She pressed her ear to the door to make sure Nurse Winthrop had gone, then she went to sit on the bed next to her mom. The whimpering had finally stopped, and she sighed. "Mom?"

Mrs. Demming's eyes fluttered for an instant. Already they were glazed from the medication. "Oh Maddie, I'm so glad you're here!"

"Mom, it was just a dream, you know. You just try to go back to sleep. I'll stay with you, okay?"

"Okay. Goodnight, Maddie," Mrs. Demming's voice trailed off. "Not a dream, not a d..."

"Night, Mom." Madison watched until finally a deep sleep settled across her mom's features. She knew it was a false sleep, brought on by the shot the nurse gave her, and that worried her. What was in those shots? What were they doing to her mom? What long term effect would there be? But most important of all, why was her mother having such horrible nightmares? She thought all that was left behind in Boston when her father had insisted she accompany her mom to Fisherman's Haven. He'd told Madison that having her along would speed up her recovery, but the recovery wasn't speeding up. It was going the other way. It was going downhill. It was getting worse. Not only was Madison's mom having the same horrible nightmares she was having in Boston, but here she was having them all the time. She was now beginning to hear things. And see things. There was always this dark shadow of a man in her dream who was coming through her room to kill her. But there was never anyone or anything in the room. She was also hearing the crying of a baby. Madison knew her mom was imagining little Zane crying because she was missing him so much herself. There were some moments when she was nearly sleeping, that she thought she heard the crying of a baby herself.

And now sitting by her mom's bedside watching her sleep, her face relaxed and beautiful, the dark brown tendrils of loose hair caressing the sides of her face, Madison began to wonder. If she herself was thinking she was hearing the crying of a baby— was there really a baby crying? And if there really was a real crying baby — was there really a man in the dark shadows that was *really* there to kill her mom?

She shuddered and looked quickly around. And then a horrible, frightening thought filled her entire being. She was scared to death that maybe what her mom was saying *was* the truth and Madison, like everyone else, was shunting it aside, not really wanting to believe her. And if it *was* true, what was she going to do? Was there anything she could do? Could she tell her father? Would he begin to think that Madison was just as crazy as her mom? Or would he believe her?

Madison gulped hard at the reality of it all. Plucking up her courage, she forced herself to get off the bed and look around the room. She moved slowly at first, looking over the photos that were there, picking one up and planting a kiss on the face of her mom and then her dad. But there was nothing. Nothing was moved, nothing was missing. Nothing was different.

Madison turned the light on in the next room. Her mom's sitting room. What a beautiful room! Soft pastel lavender wallpaper with a floor rug of muted lavender flowers with an ivory background. The settee against one wall was flanked by small oval tables piled high with fresh flowers delivered every week by the local florist. There were several chairs, a large ottoman and a coffee table. Several large tapestries mounted on the walls softened the harsh squareness of the room. All was quiet. All was as it always was.

Madison turned off the light and once more went to sit on the bed. She gently moved the lock of hair from her mom's forehead and kissed her. Her mom sighed lightly and smiled.

"Goodnight, Mom. I love you." She turned out the lights, softly closed the door and returned to her room. Despite the lateness, despite the hour, despite the fact that she had school in the morning, Madison Demming sat awake on her bed with all the lights blazing, scared to death and thinking of the possibilities.

Chapter Three

It seemed the arrival of Madison Demming had been the herald of winter. From that first day she'd walked past the boys with her icy stare, the winds blew colder. The nights faded to dawns of thick frosts that finally put an end to the last of the fall flowers and leaves on the trees. And the shock of seeing her with Zola Dostoevsky was the final straw. Within days, a blustering wind brought in a smattering of snow that soon melted, leaving everything brown and dying, and the cold smell of winter was in the air. Several weeks later, the weather worsened. The wind howled and whistled through the trees blowing thick giant snowflakes of the first real snowstorm in every direction. Temperatures plummeted to the low teens and it seemed all the goose down in the world couldn't quell the chill that penetrated every nook and cranny, every bone and joint in Fisherman's Haven.

Kurt and Willie were finishing their homework Friday evening when the storm began. By the next day they were so busy shoveling paths around the neighborhood that it was late Sunday afternoon before they were able to finally make it to Mrs. Hendicott's path. By that time, the howling wind had blown drifts across her sidewalk and the snow had accumulated to more than fifteen inches. The boys were exhausted by the time they reached the porch.

"Man, we'll never do this again!" Willie exclaimed throwing the last load from his shovel with a heavy grunt.

"What's that?"

"Leave Mrs. Hendicott for last. Next time we come down and do her path first."

"I agree. Hey," Kurt said. He turned to stare at the closed door. "Something's wrong."

"What makes you say that?" Willie leaned against the porch post.

"Usually by now Mrs. Hendicott has the door open and we can smell cookies baking."

"Geez!" Willie spun around and stared at the closed door. "You're right. We'd better get in there and check."

They cleared off the steps and entered the porch. There they stomped off the excess snow and removed their coats and boots. Using the spare key, they let themselves in. The door closed with an audible *'click'* behind them and immediately that skin crawling feeling that something was wrong hit them. The house was dark inside with a profound stillness that heightened the ticking of the grandfather clock in the parlor. No enticing aroma of fresh cookies or anything else cooking. No familiar warm glow of a fire from the fireplace in the parlor. Even the pattering paws and purring were gone. Something was definitely wrong. Even when Mrs. Hendicott was gone shopping or visiting, she always left the hall light on.

"Mrs. Hendicott! You home?" Willie called out. He edged down the darkened hall, but there was no answer.

"Hey, Mrs. Hendicott!" Kurt shouted. He turned on the hall light and started for the kitchen. At the sound of their voices, several cats bounded from the parlor mewing incessantly. Several slinked tiger-like down the stairs. It was only then the boys heard the muffled sobs coming from upstairs.

"*OH NO!*" Kurt bolted up the stairs two at a time, Willie right behind him.

They followed the sobs, and Kurt now knew they were coming from Mrs. Hendicott's bedroom. He'd been there not so long ago. It was a beautifully wallpapered room with a thick flowered carpet and frilly lace curtains which hung from the arched windows that circled the rounded sitting area. A large oak bed with matching bureau, nightstands and large armoire filled the space of the main room. Within the sitting room stood a small writing desk where a sheaf of monogrammed writing paper and matching envelopes lay next to the crystal hurricane lamp. Two balloon backed chairs of polished wood and mauve cushions, flanked the desk. Near a window, a rocking chair with an embroidered footstool near a small table, completed the furnishings in the room.

Their hearts thumping madly, they breached the top of the stairs and ran down the dark hall.

The door was open and they came to an abrupt halt. They squinted into the darkened room, horrified to find Mrs. Hendicott, a shadow in the darkness, sitting on the floor near the foot of the bed, the blankets and pillows all askew. Cradled in her arms was Missy. Kurt turned on the overhead light.

"Mrs. Hendicott!" Willie raced over to her.

"What...what happened?" Kurt knelt down beside her. Mrs. Hendicott was shaking from head to toe and her face, already swollen from tears, was a terrible ashen color.

She looked up at the boys and tried to speak but the words caught in her throat. Tears rolled down her cheeks, filling the lenses of her glasses until she couldn't see at all. It was then that Willie realized that Missy was not moving.

"Mrs. Hendicott!" He put an arm around her thin shoulders. "Are you all right?"

"It...it's my M... M... Missy," she stuttered. "She's gone!"

"Was there an accident?" Kurt asked.

"No...no...no accident," she cried shaking her head.

"What...what happened?" Willie asked.

"She.....she just....I was making my bed....my poor Missy, she came into the room and....and she was walking funny....so I got down here....here...to hold her and....she....she crawled into my lap.....and she purred for a minute....then...then...OH!"

"Mrs. Hendicott. We're really sorry," Willie said. He put a hand on top of Mrs. Hendicott's hand, the one that rested against Missy's head. "She was probably hurting or something. She probably knew she was going to die and she came to tell you that everything was all right, you know?"

"I....I think she did. She was my favorite. She was my first you know? Did I ever tell you that?" Mrs. Hendicott wiped her face with the back of her hand.

"Here," Kurt reached up to the bed side and grabbed the box of tissues.

"Thank you dear. But you may be right. She was just like a person to me. She knew when I was sad and would come and lay with me on the bed and nudge me with her cold little nose. And she knew when I was happy because she was such a stinker then. Always wanting to play and get into mischief."

"Well, she was a good little cat, that's for sure," Kurt said.

"I know." Mrs. Hendicott started crying all over again.

"Look, do you want us to do something for you? Call someone?" Willie asked.

"I...I suppose you should. Next to the phone in the hall is a rolodex and the number for Serena Pratt. She's the woman I take my cats to....she's the vet I go to..." her voice trailed back into tears.

"Don't worry. We'll take care of everything," Kurt said. With a nod to Willie he left and returned a half hour later carrying a tray of hot tea. When he got there he found that Willie had taken Missy and laid her on her blanket bed that Mrs. Hendicott always kept on the edge of her own bed. Willie helped Mrs. Hendicott up and she was now sitting in her rocking chair near the window staring at the lifeless form of her Missy.

"Here," Kurt set the tray down and poured a cup of hot tea. "I thought this would help. I phoned Dr. Pratt and she's coming right over. I told her to just come on up. Is that all right?"

"That is fine, thank you Kurt. You and Willie….goodness I don't know what I would do without you both!" She cried some more.

"Stop crying for a moment and sip that tea. It will make you feel better," Kurt said. "I hope you don't mind but I also called a friend of ours to come on over. She's a cat lover just like you. When we told her about you she was so excited and wanted to meet you. She's coming over too. Is that all right? Her name is Mai Su McKnight and she's really nice. She can help with taking care of the rest of your cats until you're able."

"That….that is so kind of you both. I don't know how to thank you…how to…"

"Never mind about all that now," Willie said. "Oh, here's someone now."

Mai Su McKnight peeked around the corner of the door and raised her eyebrows. "Is it okay to come in?"

"Hey, Mai Su!" Both Kurt and Willie called out relieved that someone else was there to help.

"Yes, come in my dear. Kurt and Willie have told me all about you. I am so grateful that you were able to come to help," Mrs. Hendicott said between sniffles.

"Hey! I'm only too happy to help. When they told me what happened I rushed right over. Don't worry," Mai Su grinned when she saw the looks on the boys' faces, "I ran instead of taking my Geo. It would probably get stuck in this snow tonight anyway. Besides, it's not that far. I see you have tons of little cute critters around. Just tell me what you want me to do. I have no problem petting them or brushing them, and I even do litter boxes!" Mai Su smiled.

"You are such a dear. Please make yourself at home in the kitchen. They have not been fed yet and oh dear....there you are!" She looked to see Serena Pratt come into the room.

"My dear Mrs. Hendicott. I am so sorry for your loss." Dr. Pratt went to the bed and stroked Missy verifying she was gone, then she went to Mrs. Hendicott.

"Thank you dear. She was my favorite you know."

"Yes I know. I will take good care of her. I will call you later to make final arrangements, is that all right?" Dr. Pratt said taking Mrs. Hendicott's hand.

"Yes. Yes that will be fine. A day or two will be soon enough."

"Then I will go. Take care of her won't you?" Dr. Pratt glanced to Willie, Kurt and Mai Su.

"Don't worry, we will," Mai Su said. "I'll walk you out and go to feed the others." Mai Su and Serena Pratt left, followed closely by scurrying little feet.

"Mai Su is cool. She likes to take charge, be the leader, you know?" Willie said with a grin to Mrs. Hendicott.

"So what are you planning to do with her? Bury her or have her cremated?" Kurt asked.

"Kurt!" Willie punched him in the arm. "Geez, let her have a breath will you?"

"Sorry! I didn't mean to sound so callous, but she has to decide."

"What would you do, if you were in my shoes, losing the best friend you've ever had?" Mrs. Hendicott peered at them through watery eyes.

"Well, I know I'd want to be cremated," Willie said. "Here, give me those." Willie reached for Mrs. Hendicott's glasses and grabbed a fresh tissue to clean them.

"Yeah me too," Kurt agreed.

"Why?" asked Mrs. Hendicott. "Thank you dear," she replaced her glasses.

"Well look at it this way, Mrs. Hendicott. If you bury Missy, you'll only get to see her during the summer. In the winter she'll be under tons of snow and you'll never get to see her. If she's cremated, you can keep her urn of ashes on the fireplace mantle next to that picture of your grandfather and see her every day!" Kurt exclaimed.

"What a wonderful idea. I believe that is what I will do."

"Okay then," Mai Su came into the room followed by the soft sound of pattering paws, "no more of this talk. I've put on a quick supper, only a can of soup and some sandwiches, and we will all go down. I don't want to hear any protests, Mrs. Hendicott. The rest of these guys still need you too, you know." Mai Su swept her hand to indicate the seven cats that followed her mewing into the bedroom.

"You're right, young lady." Mrs. Hendicott wiped her tears, put on a brave face and reached for the arm Willie offered. "Help me up, won't you Willie, dear?"

"Sure, come on lean on me. I'm pretty tough," Willie grinned.

"We all are pretty tough after hauling Teddy around for hours," Mai Su smiled and led the way down. "Careful, these little guys are everywhere!"

The soup and toasted cheese sandwiches were just what everyone needed. Kurt retrieved the tea tray from the bedroom and while Mai Su warmed the pot, the boys helped Mrs. Hendicott into the parlor and started the fire in the fireplace.

"So, did you know that someone moved into the Towering Pines Manor?" Mai Su said breaking the silence when she entered the room. She set the tray down and poured the tea.

"Yes, but I have been so busy here that I haven't ventured out much," Mrs. Hendicott said sipping the hot tea. "And with this storm! Goodness! I haven't even gotten any shopping done!"

"I can do that for you tomorrow after school if you can manage that long," Mai Su offered.

"Yes I can. I'll wait for you with a list tomorrow," Mrs. Hendicott smiled at her. "So who is in the manor?"

"Some new family from *Boston,*" Mai Su said haughtily, "as Miss Snob would say."

"Boston? Fisherman's Haven is a far cry, financially speaking, from Boston," Mrs. Hendicott remarked.

"Sure is and Miss Snob lets everyone know every chance she gets. What I don't get," Mai Su continued oblivious of the throat clearing, the coughing and the nodding heads from Kurt and Willie trying to get her attention, "is what is she doing hanging around with that eighth grader, Zola Dostoevsky? I mean, they are so direct opposites and can't have a possible thing in common and....what? What?"

"Geez, don't you ever take a breath?" Kurt cried.

"Course not. You know I'm going to tell it like it is," she replied. Mrs. Hendicott smiled.

"So this Miss Snob of yours, who is she?" she asked.

"Her name," said Willie almost dreamily, "is Madison Demming. Don't you think that's a really cool name? Madison Demming!"

"Oh my God! You like her!" Mai Su shouted with a screeching giggle that sent Little Santa, a chubby bright red tabby, jumping from her lap.

"Do not!"

"Do too, else why would you think anything about that snob is cool?"

"Well, she really is. She has long beautiful hair and when she's not wearing those stupid sunglasses, she has the greenest eyes and her complexion is so smooth and..."

"Oh it's beautiful hair? It looks like mud brown to me," giggled Mai Su. "and smooth....."

"Well it's true, it has those like streaked highlights and...."

"Shut up, Will, you're only digging the hole deeper," Kurt laughed.

"You should talk. You're the one that has the hots for Dusty!" Willie retorted.

"So what?"

"Oh my God! You guys are so mental!" Mai Su laughed.

Mrs. Hendicott smiled. It was nice having the distraction. "So there's a new girl in the manor house? It's said to be haunted, you know."

That shut them up in an instant and they turned wide-eyed at Mrs. Hendicott.

"Haunted?" Willie gulped.

"The manor house is haunted?" Mai Su blinked several times.

"Oh yes. Has been for...oh...several hundred years. Don't tell me none of you have heard the stories?" Mrs. Hendicott set her cup down and it was immediately pounced upon by two scrambling cats. They knocked it over on the tray and bounded away behind the sofa chasing each other obviously feeling much better now that they were fed and warm.

"No. Course nobody has lived there for years so I suppose no one talks about it anymore," Mai Su said.

"And Willie and I have only lived here for a few years so we don't know anything about it." Kurt set his cup down, too. "So tell us about it."

"Oh, I'm not so sure I remember all the details."

"Nonsense, you have the keenest memory of anybody I know," Willie cried. Mrs. Hendicott beamed.

Chapter Four

It turned out that Mrs. Hendicott really couldn't remember much that day. Willie, Kurt and Mai Su put it down to sadness over the loss of her Missy cat. Besides, it was getting late, so Mai Su cleaned up the dishes while the boys stoked the fire in the grate. Mai Su stopped to see Mrs. Hendicott every day after school for the next week to help her and just make sure everything was all right. The boys stopped several times and cleared the sidewalk and helped with trash removal and other small chores.

Otherwise, each day was the same. Standing near the fence between the two schools, Kurt and Willie watched Madison Demming talking and actually giggling with Zola Dostoevsky. Each day after school the girls would meet and walk together around the corner where, unknown to everyone, the black Chrysler would be waiting for them. Yet despite those seemingly happy moments, Madison Demming's face soon developed a haggard look. The puffy little pouchy bags beneath her eyes got darker. Her head wasn't held so high anymore and her chin had drooped dramatically towards her chest. And then she was actually seen dozing in class. Each day the boy's curiosity grew. By the time the Saturday after Thanksgiving rolled around they were sufficiently irritated with the whole situation. Well, Kurt was. He just couldn't see how Zola could be friends with the snob.

He was pretty quiet early that Saturday morning, the whole time they were shoveling the sidewalk. Willie looked at him sideways every so often, but he didn't intrude. He could see that something was weighing on Kurt's mind and Kurt would let him know when the time was right.

Tossing shovel load after shovel load, Kurt's mind was running in circles. He really liked Zola. Perhaps more than he wanted to ever admit out loud. He just couldn't see how such a pretty, sweet girl like Zola would have anything in common with – well with – Madison Demming. They were just putting their shovels away when Kurt blurted out, "I think we should do something about that."

"What! About what?" Willie asked, taken completely by surprise.

"Oh, sorry. I was thinking that maybe we should go pay a visit to the ice cream shop today, you know, just to …oh….have…some ice cream!"

"So obvious!" Willie laughed. "You just want to go to see Zola, don't you?"

"Well sure, and to try to find out what her and Miss Snob have in common," Kurt replied.

"Do you think that's any of your business?"

"No, not exactly, but it sure is bugging me. And doesn't it seem strange that Miss Snob has been caught sleeping in class? And that she looks like she's not sleeping …..like she has some night job or something?"

"Sure I noticed. I noticed that a week ago. There's something different…like I don't know how to explain it. I don't think it's that she's snobby. I think, well, I think there might be something wrong. It's almost like she's scared."

"Scared! Scared of what!" Kurt exclaimed.

"I don't know. But I'd sure like to know. I mean if she's scared because other kids are threatening her or harassing her or something…"

"Now who's butting in on none of his business."

"Well you're the one who brought it up!" Willie countered.

"Geez, don't get touchy with me. I know you like Miss Snob even if no one else does."

"How can I like someone when I don't even know someone? Don't be stupid. So, how much money you got in your pocket?" Willie changed the subject. He watched Kurt pull off his glove and finger the quarters pressed inside.

"Two bucks."

"You have more than that!" Willie cried. "We just cleared three sidewalks!"

"Well sure, but I'm not going to spend all my snow shoveling money on ice cream!" Kurt cried back.

"But you're the one who wants to go! Okay, okay. I'll buy. *This* time!" Willie laughed.

"So what do you think is going on with those two?" Kurt asked after shouting in the door to his dad that they were leaving.

"I don't know. You know girls. They are weird as weird can be," Willie shrugged. A few minutes later he pulled open the door to the ice cream shop and continued. "One day they are your good friends and the next day they want to be something else. Take Melissa Drury for instance. Never spoke to either of us until that day you rescued her sister Sasha from the ice. Then, suddenly she was hanging around being a pest. What do.... hey?" Willie pulled back when Kurt punched him in the arm. He followed Kurt's nod to a corner table where Madison sat with Zola, their heads so close their foreheads were touching. Madison was red- faced and puffy- eyed. She kept dabbing at her eyes with a tissue. They both looked up when the boys entered the ice cream shop and Madison quickly turned her face away. For just an instant, Zola stared at them, an almost pleading look in her eyes, then she turned back to Madison and was insistent that Madison do something. Madison's head flew back and forth just as insistent that she not.

"Zola, customers," Sergei Dostoevsky called out.

"Yes, Papa," Zola answered. She said one last thing to Madison before she walked towards Kurt and Willie.

"Hello, Willie. Hello, Kurt."

"Hi, Zola," Kurt said. "Came in for a dish of ice cream. Only have a couple of dollars so whatever that will get us." Zola smiled.

"It will be just enough." She left and returned later with two bowls heaped with a rich vanilla topped with chunks of dark chocolate crunch.

"This looks like a new flavor," Kurt said stuffing a spoonful in his mouth. "Ummmmm!"

"It is. Papa mixed it up special after your counterfeiter episode. He calls it Crumbling Cliffs after Pirate's Cove! See there is the chocolate on the ice cream to look like the cliffs and the crunch to look like little rocks."

"So cool! Tell him thanks!" Willie grinned.

"I will." She cast a concerned look over her shoulder and hurried back to Madison. A few snatches of urgent conversation, a quick look back at the boys, and soon Zola was tugging Madison by the arm towards them.

"Ummm this is the be…." Kurt raised his eyes over the bowl. "Oh, hi."

"Kurt, Willie, this is Madison Demming. She is my friend," said Zola.

"Oh, well, hi," Willie muttered. "I mean if it's okay to talk to you at all without your permission… ouch!" Kurt kicked him beneath the table

"I…I…I am really sorry for that first day. It's just that nobody understands what it's like moving to a new town and being the new kid and having everyone stare at you and oh….I just hate it here!" Madison began to cry.

"Oh, geez," Kurt rolled his eyes and Willie laughed.

Madison quickly wiped the tears and snapped at Zola, "See! I told you! They're just stupid boys!"

"Man! Have you got us wrong! We both were the new kid at one time or another. First me, then Kurt came a couple years ago. Now, you. Don't beat us up cause we know exactly how you feel, and believe us, it does get better. Especially when you find a good friend, right Kurt?"

"Right!"

Madison tossed her head, her hair swirling away from her face. She gave a beseeching look to Zola. Zola nodded slightly and motioned for her to sit down. Madison hesitated, then shrugged her shoulders, took a deep breath and pushed her way into the booth next to Willie. Zola sat next to Kurt. Willie pulled himself closer to the wall, thought better of it, and moved back so his arm was touching Madison's arm.

"You have to tell them what is happening, Madison. I told you before, if anyone can help you, these two can." Zola reached for Madison's hand.

"I...I don't know. It's all so strange," Madison said. She had regained some of her composure, and the arrogant look returned to her features even as tears threatened to spill. She looked quickly from Kurt to Willie and then back to Zola. Since her arrival in Fisherman's Haven, the only person she ever talked to was Zola. And that was only since that day when Zola had found her on a swing at the small park on Lexington Street crying her eyes out. It was then that Zola told Madison of her first days at a new school, hardly able to speak the American language and not knowing what to do or what to expect from a new country let alone a new school. Madison had, for the first time in her life, felt sorry for someone other than herself. She'd been having such a personal pity party that she had never thought about how it felt for anyone else around her. Yet her situation was different. And when Zola told her she understood about her mom , understood about the crazy noises and voices before Madison ever told her anything about Towering Pines Manor, it was then she knew she could confide in Zola and call her friend. But now, sitting here with these two boys, Madison was having second thoughts.

"Well, we won't know if we can help if you don't tell us what is going on and for pete's sake, don't cry!" Kurt hissed. And that was when Madison burst into uncontrollable sobs.

"Oh geez!" Kurt scrambled for the napkins at the nearby table.

"It's horrible! Just horrible! Moving here, moving in that house, the thing with my mother, everything!" Madison blurted.

"Zola!" her father called.

"Yes, Papa?" Zola jumped from the seat.

"Take your sister out to the back to play in the snow. The sun is warm and she is under your mother's foot."

"Yes, Papa. Can you come with me? I have to take Zeva outside for a while."

"Sure. It's nice and sunny and she'll have lots of fun." Kurt smiled at her.

They waited for several minutes while Zola dressed Zeva, who, typical of a five year old, fidgeted and giggled Zola into exasperation. Then they trudged through the snow into the back yard. The sun was warm and inviting and the snow was soft and sticky. "Here, Zeva," Zola started a snowball. "Roll that and when you get three of them, we will build a snowman."

Everyone went to sit down on the benches near the back porch and watched as Zeva rolled in the snow making snow angels, then set to work rolling balls for her snowman.

"So to get back to your situation, Madison," Willie prompted.

"Well, now that I've had time to think, I really don't know that you boys can do anything for me." Madison had regained control of herself once more. She stared straight ahead, her nose in the air.

"Oh, please, Madison, please," Zola protested. She looked helplessly from Kurt to Willie and back to Madison.

"Look, if you don't want our help, there's nothing much we can do about it," Kurt said with disgust. He went to help

Zeva roll snowballs. After several moments of silence, Madison turned sideways on the bench, away from Willie when tears once more filled her eyes. Willie shook his head and followed Kurt.

"Madison, please," Zola pleaded. "These boys are really good. I told you about how they rescued Teddy Rigetta, didn't I? You have to know they saved his life, and his girlfriend's too, at the risk of their own!"

"They are just boys! You saw how they laughed and joked about this!" Madison folded her arms. She blinked quickly to stop the tears once more. "I thought the way you talked about them that they were much more mature than…than…just boys!"

"Well, of course, they *are* just boys. But they are boys that are willing to help, if you would only let them. Oh please, just give them a chance!" Zola cried. "You have to tell someone!"

Madison turned to her friend. She immediately felt sorry that she had embarrassed Zola in front of her friends. After all, Zola was the only person in Fisherman's Haven that had any clue what was going on at Towering Pines Manor. She was the only person in Fisherman's Haven that didn't laugh at her, didn't shun her and was willing to help. She owed her at least a try. "All right, I guess I can show them around the house."

"Great, we'll tell them when they finish the snowman," Zola smiled. They sat and watched while Kurt and Willie helped Zeva roll two giant snowballs then lift the small one onto the big one. "Grab that little one Zeva," Kurt picked her up and she put it on for the head. "Now run inside and ask mama for a long carrot and two really big olives!"

"All right!" Zeva ran through the backdoor into the kitchen and was out in a flash waving a carrot in one hand and two large black olives in the other. She stumbled in the snow and the carrot went flying in the air while her hand tightened and she squished the two large olives to a pulp. She started to cry when she saw the crushed olives.

[29]

"Hey!" Kurt exclaimed, rescuing the carrot and Zeva from the snow. "Those are perfect! Look how they look when you put them on your snowman! Two perfect fat, gobby, watery eyes!" Zeva laughed and blinked the tears away.

"Time to come in," Zola's mother called from the door. "Time for a nap!" Zeva pouted.

"We can make another snowman next time, okay?" Willie comforted her.

"I suppose I should go. I have to help in the shop." Zola rose to leave.

"Richard, pick me up. I'm at the ice cream shop!" Madison slammed her cell phone shut.

"Little rude aren't you?" Willie asked.

"Rude? He's just an employee. It's expected," Madison replied. They walked in silence back into the shop and Zola brought her sister upstairs for her nap. Kurt and Willie followed Madison outside and waited on the sidewalk. Why, they didn't know. An awkward silence fell between them. A moment later, Zola met them outside tugging her coat on.

"Papa said I could come. I am so excited!" she cried.

"Come? Come where?" Kurt asked.

"Oh, didn't Madison tell? She said she would show you around the house and see what you can determine. And I'm coming with you!"

"Wonderful. At least I won't be alone with these two guys," Madison retorted.

"Oh, now we're guys, not boys?" Kurt sneered.

"Did we agree or something?" Willie frowned at Kurt.

"Well? Would you at least look?" Madison retorted.

"Geez, you make us sound like scoundrels or something," Kurt said. He cast a disgusted look at Willie. "And what are we supposed to be looking for?"

But there was no time to argue or explain. At that moment the black Chrysler cruised to a smooth stop and Richard quickly emerged from behind the wheel to open the back door.

"These are friends, Richard, they are coming with me."

"Yes, Miss Demming." The shock that Madison Demming had any friends at all was extremely well hidden on Richard's face, but Kurt caught the slight arch of his eyebrows. Once inside the car, he noticed how Richard looked more than once in his rear view mirror at them. He wondered what this Richard character was all about. Here after all, was a young man, probably in his twenties, acting as a chauffeur to a very beautiful, albeit, antagonizing young girl. He wasn't all that bad looking, either, thought Kurt. The guy had dark hair, dark eyes, almost an olive complexion, probably Italian or something like that. He had a thin moustache that lined his upper lip giving him a handsome look that girls dribble over. Kurt absentmindedly ran his finger beneath his nose, wondering when the hair on his face would grow and he'd have to start shaving. He glanced over to Willie who was sandwiched between the girls with all four of them scrunched in the back seat. Willie looked pretty happy!

They drove to Towering Pines Manor in awkward silence. The ride wasn't very long , but it was smooth and comfortable as the Chrysler virtually hovered over the road, a far cry from the boys bumpy rides with Mai Su McKnight.

They drove for several blocks until the houses began to thin and empty lots and trees filled the spaces. Soon they passed the last of the houses and it wasn't long after that   the car   slowed and turned onto the private road   leading to the manor. Here the trees had been cut away from the edges for snow plowing purposes. Visible over the tops of the pines, loomed the peak of one solitary roof. A square tower of weathered rock and boarded windows rose to challenge the highest of trees for supremacy of the sky. Even the sight of that disappeared as they wove their way along the road.

It was a narrow, paved road that curved and twisted on its ascent to the top of the hill. Great pines grew on both sides of the road filling the forest with an almost impenetrable mass of hanging green boughs and dark odd shaped shadows. Even though it was early afternoon, darkness enveloped the interior of the forest. A smattering of sunlight broke through here and there where a tree had fallen or been cut away. It was an eerie ride amidst the shadows, and no one spoke at all.

The car passed through the black wrought iron gates that stood open. They were wedged back and barricaded with mounds of snow that looked like they would be that way for a long time. They circled the limestone water fountain that lay partially buried beneath a heavy blanket of snow. When Richard pulled the car to a stop and they got out, Willie, Kurt and Zola stared in awe at the Towering Pines Manor that had been so skillfully hidden all those years.

A large portico with six huge columns of white limestone supported the almost Grecian looking lintel above. The stairs were covered with a dusting of fresh snow and led towards the massive oak door of the house. Madison tossed her hair back and without a backward glance, threw open the door and just expected that Kurt, Willie and Zola were following. Not hearing footsteps behind her, she turned and shouted. "Well, come on in! Oh Agnes," she continued when a servant appeared, "these are friends of mine. We will have a snack in the dining room and then we wish to be left alone."

"Yes, Miss Demming," Agnes replied with a nod and slipped quietly away. She was an old woman with greying hair tied back in a bun behind her head. Her black soled shoes barely made a sound on the marble floor as she walked quickly towards the kitchen. Madison started towards the dining room.

"Rude!" Kurt hissed in Willie's ear from the doorway. "She is so rude!"

"I know!"

"I thought you liked her?" Kurt whispered back.

"Like or not, there's no reason to be so rude."

"So what do we do? Stay or go?"

"Well, we agreed to take a look around and that we'll do. After that, she's on her own," Willie whispered back. "And she still didn't tell us what we're supposed to be looking for!"

"I know!"

"Please, do not let her arrogance prevent you from helping her," Zola whispered, quickly closing the door. She took several tentative steps into the grand hall and stopped to stare. She shivered and her face paled. She reached back to clutch at Kurt's hand.

"What's the matter?" Kurt stepped up beside her.

"I don't like this place. There is something evil here, Kurt," Zola whispered.

"For real?" Willie moaned.

"Stop that," Kurt hissed to Willie. To Zola he said. "Come on Zola, what is it that you feel?"

"I....I don't know exactly. It's like....like...there's a struggle between the old and the new, between what has happened and what is to come....oh, I can't explain it," she cried.

Madison had stiffened and slowed down when she heard their whispers behind her. She knew what people said about her and it hurt but she didn't know what else to do about it. She turned to them and called, "Well? Are you coming? We'll eat first, then I can show you around a bit."

The boys shrugged their shoulders and followed. After walking the distance that was almost the entire length of Willie's house, they turned left into the dining room where a lunch of quartered sandwiches and fruits was already waiting. They ate in silence, Madison picking at her sandwich, choosing those quarters with the crust cut off, then very carefully selecting two small slices of melon.

Kurt met Willie's look and they both rolled their eyes. The boys quickly chewed and swallowed, eager to get out. "Well, let's get this over with," Kurt said standing up from the table.

"Come on then." Madison led the way back through to the foyer. "Okay, so you've just seen the dining room Over there," she pointed to her left, "is the sitting room. Not much in here to see." She walked over, pushed open the door and gave them enough time to poke their heads, take note of the opened drapes of the patio doors on the opposite wall, then quickly shut the door. "Over this way is the study." She went to the next door and once again pushed the door open and allowed only enough time to poke their heads in. Closing the door, she walked to the end of the room, did an abrupt right turn and stopped at a set of doors. "This set of doors is locked and leads to the wing of the house that we don't use so there's no point in bothering with them. Here," she followed along the wall, " is the solarium and you can see it leads us right back to the front door. Now, if you will come this way, we'll go on upstairs and I can show you that."

"Show us what?" Willie whispered in Kurt's ear. "She doesn't give us time to look at anything!"

"I can see why everyone calls her Miss Snob!" Kurt whispered back.

Madison stiffened once more, for the whispers, no matter how softly uttered, reached her ears. She hesitated only for a moment. She knew what the other kids called her behind her back but that was something she had to live with. She would rather live with that than have them know exactly what was happening at Towering Pines Manor.

She led them up the oak stairs that spiraled up to the second landing. She pointed to their left. "That way is my mother's suite which consist of her bedroom, a bathroom and her own sitting room. There's another bathroom just there. This way is my room, and these are just additional bedrooms." She pointed to the three doors that they passed along the passage to their right. "At the end of the hall here is a door that goes to the other wing of the house. I guess it wasn't original to the house when it was built, but added on when they sealed off the other wing there. Nobody has ever been in there."

"So let's go in there," Willie said.

"I don't think we're allowed," Madison said. "It's locked, just like the one downstairs."

"So what!" Anger had been building up in Kurt since that stupid smirk on Madison's face back at Zola's place. Calling them boys! Insinuating they were stupid! Worse! Untrustworthy! Well he'd just about had it with Miss Snob. He grabbed the handle with Madison's own smirky look on his face. Surprised to find it gave way when he turned it, he flung the door open and stepped into the dark hallway beyond. He spun around, hands planted on his hips, his look daring Madison to throw him out. They'd been shuffled through from room to room, from downstairs to upstairs and barely had a glimpse of anything that was there. So by this time, Kurt was pretty much out of patience.

"Thought you said it was locked?" Kurt cried.

"It…it's supposed to be. It was when we moved in here." Madison stuttered for a moment forgetting Kurt's brazen daredevil look.

Willie quickly followed Kurt inside and Zola and Madison had no choice but to follow. "Well it certainly is open now! Come on let's have a look!" A long hall stretched before them and here they could see several more rooms to the left and right and a boarded window at the end. They followed each other down the hall, checking doors as they went. Nearly all were dark with windows boarded and furniture covered in dust cloths. When they reached the end of the hall, there was another stair case on their right that led down and another closed door at a twisted angle in an alcove to their left. Willie approached the door on the left and gripped the old black iron handle, his thumb to the top latch clicking it up and down. It was unlocked.

"Well? What are you waiting for?" Madison tapped her shoe to the floor.

"Which way to go? Down the stairs over there on the right, or see what's behind door number two in this alcove?" Willie asked

"I say we go down. It should lead us back to the lower floors of the house," Zola said.

"I say we see what's behind door number two!" Kurt exclaimed. He pushed off Willie's hand from the handle, grabbed it and pulled it open before anyone could protest.

A blast of cold air hit them and they found themselves staring at yet another flight of stairs, narrow and winding and dark. Here, at the twist of the alcove, the light from the hallway beyond did not reach. Everyone stood motionless, as if glued to the floor. Icy drafts of air brushed by sending shivers through them. Zola inched back and Madison began to say something but Kurt pushed forward mounting the first five stairs, then turned to them and said, "Well?" Hesitantly, they followed Kurt, Zola clinging to the back of his shirt with Madison scrunched at her side, shoulder to wall, with Willie at the back.

"Kurt!" she whispered in his ear. "I don't like this, we must turn back."

SLAM..........

went the door behind them, enveloping them in complete darkness.

Chapter Five

Madison's breath caught in her throat and her whole body stiffened as panic overwhelmed her in the darkness. Terrified, she screamed and shoved Kurt headlong up the stairs. Zola cried out and shrank against the wall out of the way as Madison shoved against her, and slammed into Willie, driving him backwards against the door. Willie caught his balance and shouted, "Shut up!" to Madison and Kurt pushed past them all to get to the door. "Come on Will, someone must have hit it!"

"Not me!" Zola's voice trembled.

"Certainly not me!" Madison screeched. "I was right behind *you*!"

"Well it wasn't me either," Willie mumbled in the darkness rubbing his shoulder. "Come on, grab that handle."

But hard as they tried, the door would not budge. They jiggled the handle up and down and sideways, tugged and pulled and banged around it with their fists to dislodge the lock.

"Willie stop! Stop, stop ,stop! If we pull the darn thing off entirely we'll never get out," Kurt said leaning back rubbing his sore hands.

"You're right," Willie groaned.

"What! What are you saying! Are we stuck in here? Help!" Madison bumped against the walls, knocking into everyone in her attempt to get to the door.

"Shut up!" Kurt told her again.

"Don't you tell me to shut up!" Madison shouted.

"Shhhh! Did you hear that?" Zola whispered. Everyone grew deathly silent.

"Hear what?" they whispered.

"Listen!" Zola whispered.

They stood still, ears pricked to hear what Zola had heard. They strained their ears and squinted into the darkness.

"What? What is it?" Willie asked. "I don't hear anything!"

"Do you hear it?" Fear gripped Zola. She fought to control the trembling, the sick feeling in the pit of her stomach. She felt trapped in a world where no one would ever know or understand. The desire to scream, to run, to be done with it all was overwhelming , but the need to know and understand and set them free was overpowering. She turned slowly when the sound of footsteps approached from above. "It's coming from up there!"

"I hear it!" Madison croaked. She gripped Zola's arm and pulled her with her inching her way down the stairs then hugged the space between Kurt and Willie. She was shaking from head to foot.

"We don't hear anything!" Willie cried.

"It's a rustling sound....like....like the sound clothes make when brushed against something!" Zola whispered. "Someone is coming!"

"I hear it! Footsteps!" Madison whispered. "It's coming from there! From up the stairs!" She pointed in the darkness.

Willie held out his wrist and pressed the tiny button that illuminated his watch. Both Madison and Zola screamed when the tiny beam of green light pierced the darkness. The mysterious noise coming down the stairs stopped, and a mist like a breath in the freeze of winter lingered in the green glow of the watch. It swirled and writhed as if in agony before evaporating up the winding stairs.

No one spoke. No one dared breathe. No one dared move.

"Okay, that can be explained," Kurt whispered, breaking the silence, mindful of the hairs on the back of his neck standing straight up.

"It's her!" Zola whispered. "She's here!"

"It's nobody, Zola." Willie pushed Madison from his side. "It's so bloody cold in here it was just our breath, that's all."

"Come on, let's try this....." Willie had turned to grip the door handle once more and this time the latch moved easily and he was able to push the door open. "There, see? I told you. It was only jammed is all. Come on, let's get out of here. It's really cold."

They tumbled from the stairs and the boys slammed the door tightly shut behind them. The color had drained from Madison's face and she leaned heavily on Zola. Cold and shaken, unsure of what had just happened, nobody spoke. They followed Madison silently back to her room. She threw herself on her bed and pulled the quilts around her to stop shivering. "What was all that?" she cried. "I told you! I told you there's something wrong with this place!"

"It's her," Zola said again. Her face was a ghostly white and she stared wide- eyed about the room.

"Who? Who is it supposed to be, Zola," Willie demanded angrily. "For crying out loud, it was just our breath. Don't start making up some ghostly white spirit mumbo jumbo and scaring the wits out of everyone."

"I'm not trying to scare anyone, but I know what I saw. I know what I felt, Willie. There is something wrong in this house, something that happened in the past. Maybe something that is going to happen in the future. I cannot determine yet. The feelings and images are so mixed together, but I know what I saw," Zola swallowed. Her eyes rested on Kurt's face, pleading for him to believe her.

"You are such a ...." Willie began but Kurt cut him off.

"Stop it! Everyone stop it. We said we'd check out the place and you should have told us what is going on here. As a matter of fact, you probably still should. There's a logical explanation for everything. We just have to investigate further. And this stupid tour of yours was no help. Opening a door and shutting it in our faces before we could get a good look around. That was no help at all. But I do know who can help."

"Who?" everyone asked.

"Mrs. Hendicott. Remember Willie? That night that Missy.....well.... that night. She said something to Mai Su and us that Towering Pines Manor was haunted."

"*Haunted*? Haunted, and I am living in this place? Oh my God!" Madison cried and pulled the quilts tighter. Zola shivered and drew closer to Madison.

"Look, she couldn't remember much then, but maybe she can tell us something about the place now," Kurt added.

"It's worth a try," Willie admitted. "It'll give us a starting place anyway."

"All right. Then let's go there," Madison threw back the quilts. "I want to know what is going on here because if it is haunted I am not staying here another night!"

"Then let's get going." They followed Willie downstairs where Madison told Agnes to have Richard bring the car around. She was still shaking when the car pulled up, but was determined to find out the truth. The Chrysler was quiet as it rolled over the snow covered blacktop, through the darkness of the towering pines and back towards Fisherman's Haven. The boys gave him the directions and soon they were parked on Mrs. Hendicott's street.

"Wait for us," Madison told Richard.

The girls followed Kurt and Willie into the porch where they removed their coats and boots. Willie knocked on the door and they could hear the scraping of a chair and shuffling of slipper covered feet on the hardwood floor. The door opened and a head of ruffled silver hair peeked through.

"Oh my goodness!" Mrs. Hendicott exclaimed and threw the door wide open. "Kurt and Willie! I was thinking about you boys! Oh, I see you have company! Come in, come in!" She led them forward.

Madison followed behind Zola and squealed. "Cats! Get them out of here! Get them away from me!"

"Why? Are you afraid of cats?" Willie asked her.

"No, I just don't like them. And I changed my mind. What is she going to tell us anyway?" Madison backed up against the wall. She pushed a cat away with her foot and mumbled under her breath, " I don't like this stupid idea of coming here and talking to this senile old lady anymore!"

"Just shut up, Madison." Kurt was getting pretty disgusted having to tell her to shut up over and over.

"Why don't you children just sit and…"

"I am not a child!" Madison shouted, hands on her hips.

"I…I…I didn't mean to insinuate you were," Mrs. Hendicott replied.

"Oh, *shut up*, Madison," Kurt said again. "It's all right, Mrs. Hendicott. We'll go sit down."

She nodded appreciatively to Kurt then retreated to the kitchen. Kurt gave Willie that look that said 'I think we made a mistake,' and Zola grasped Madison by the hand and tugged her into the parlor.

But Madison was angry now. She pulled her arm away from Zola and turned on Kurt. "I don't know who you think you are, Kurt! Talking to me like that. What do you think we are going to accomplish here? She's just an old lady, probably senile and everything. And all these cats! God how disgusting! These dirty little stinky creatures….get away from me!" Madison shoved her foot forward thrusting a small black cat away from her.

"Ahem!" Mrs. Hendicott coughed from the door. "Here we are! Please come in and sit down everyone."

Zola pulled Madison to the sofa. Again Madison kicked at one of the cats, this time it was Alexander the Great, who, antisocial as he was, had permitted his curiosity to get the best of him. He took a tentative sniff at Madison's toes. She kicked him away and shrank back on the sofa. Alexander the Great

[41]

screeched a terrifying and piercing cry of anger, hissed at Madison and stalked away, his tail twitching back and forth.

Everything in the room seemed to stop instantly. Zola stared unbelievingly at the way Madison was behaving. Mrs. Hendicott stopped midway at placing the tray on the table and followed Alexander the Great with a concerned eye. Kurt stared open-mouthed and Willie clamped a hand over his face. Willie shook his head. He'd had enough.

"That's it!" He jumped up and grabbed Madison roughly by the arm. He pulled her into the front porch and slammed the door behind them so hard, the latch failed to catch and the door creaked open behind him. He was seething angry and it was a rare moment when Willie lost his temper. He thrust his finger in Madison's face. She backed up out of the way. "Look! I don't know who the hell you think you are and I really don't give one damn how much money you have or how beautiful you are. There is no way anyone, not even you, is going to talk to and treat Mrs. Hendicott like that. Not here, not anywhere, do you understand!" Willie shouted.

Madison's eyes blazed and she thrust her hands to her hips. "I…"

"Shut up! You don't get to come here and disrespect one of the nicest people in the world. You don't get to come here and hurt her animals and disrespect her home. As a matter of fact, I don't know why we brought you here in the first place. You are nothing but a snobby witch just like everyone says. And as far as that help we promised? Well! That's over with. Go get your help somewhere else. Go on, get your coat and boots on and tell Richard to take you home because you're not welcome here anymore!" Willie left slamming the door in her face, leaving her in the porch with her mouth gaping. He stopped in the hall, leaning against the door, the anger seething in him was slow to calm.

Kurt entered the hall and waited for a couple of minutes, giving Willie the time he needed. "Thanks. That was well overdue. Come on. Our hot chocolate is getting cold."

"I am so sorry for cursing like that, but she made me so mad!" Willie took a deep breath. "Come on." They went back into the parlor. "We are so sorry, Mrs. Hendicott!" Willie cried. "Are you okay?"

"Oh, Willie dear, yes. That was so good of you to come to Alexander's rescue."

"Well, she had no right to kick him like that. So you're sure you're okay?"

"I am now," Mrs. Hendicott glanced to Alexander who had rolled to his back on the hearth rug and began licking his paws. Then her eyes inched upwards to the black urn covered with kitty paw prints that sat beneath the portrait of her grandfather on the mantle.

"Oh cool! I see you got Missy b….. what the heck are you still doing here?" Willie's tone changed to anger and the smile wiped from his face when he saw Madison inching her way back into the parlor.

She had slipped quietly through the door, closing it without a sound behind her. She crept along the hall only daring to make herself known when she couldn't hold back the sobs any longer.

"I am so sorry!" she cried when the tears spilled down her cheeks. "I didn't mean to hurt the cat! I didn't mean to be so rude! It's just that I'm so scared and all alone and I don't know where to turn, and I hate this place and all the scary things going on at the house. All the whispers and the creaking and doors slamming and…." She burst into uncontrollable sobs.

Mrs. Hendicott rose and put her arm around her. "Come and sit my dear. It is so easy to understand when one is frightened and alone how one can become angry and take it out on those around you, isn't that right boys?"

Kurt sat with an angry look on his face until the invisible hand of understanding slapped him on the forehead. He thought back to that time when he was the new kid, when he hated being there, when he was so angry he took it out on

Willie and everyone around him. He thought back to the fight and to the second chance that Willie had given him and how it turned his life around. He had unconsciously turned his hand over and was staring at the tiny scar on his thumb and he nodded. "I guess so," he said meekly. "I guess everyone deserves a second chance."

"Wha...what are you both nuts?" Willie cried. He'd been hurt and angry more than anyone because he had brought Madison into Mrs. Hendicott's house. But when he saw the tiny scar on Kurt's thumb, he, too, took a good look at the one on his thumb and finally agreed. "Okay. I guess so. But I'm not taking back anything I said in there!"

"I don't blame you. Everything you said was true." Madison accepted the tissue Zola handed her.

"Now just let me put these mugs in the microwave and we'll have some hot chocolate!" Mrs. Hendicott swept up the now cooled tray of mugs and disappeared into the kitchen, only to return with steaming mugs and a bag full of tiny marshmallows. "I think we deserve a lot of these today! So tell us what's been going on my dear!"

"I...I don't know where to start! It's all such a jumbled mess!" Madison wiped tears from her cheeks and reached for a handful of marshmallows.

"Why don't you just start at the beginning, all right?" Willie shifted on the sofa to make room for Madison. She walked past Alexander the Great who bared his teeth in a snarl and swiped at her passing feet.

"Alexander!" Mrs. Hendicott chastised.

"No, it's all right, Mrs. Hendicott. I deserved that." Madison sat down and dumped the marshmallows in her mug of chocolate.

"So tell them! Tell them everything!" Zola urged.

"Maybe you're right, Zola. After everything you've told me about them, just maybe you're right." Madison looked around the room, unsure where to start. Sighing heavily, she began. "It started about two years ago, when we still lived in

Boston. My dad is an attorney and my mom is…well…just a rich socialite I guess you would say. Two years ago my mom had a baby, my little brother Zane. It wasn't long after that things started to happen."

"What do you mean? What sort of things?" Willie asked. He threw a concerned look at Mrs. Hendicott but saw she was listening intently to Madison. He was glad. Glad she wasn't the type of person to ever hold a grudge. Glad that she was the type of person who always saw the good in people.

"Strange things like my mom starting to freak out over stupid stuff. Like my mom crying all the time and breaking down into hysterics for no reason. She started acting strange towards Zane and after a while she stopped holding him or anything. It was like she wanted nothing to do with him."

"That is strange." Kurt shot raised eye brows to Willie.

"I know. It wasn't until Agnes, our housekeeper, said something that maybe Mom was suffering from post-partum depression. You know, some women get that after they have a baby. They think they can't cope and they go through this hating their baby thing."

"Are you kidding? Is that kind of thing for real?" Kurt cried.

"Yes, there is such a thing," Mrs. Hendicott said sadly. "There are numerous cases of this type of behavior. But," she continued when she saw the frown on Kurt's face, "it doesn't happen to every woman that has a baby."

"Oh, Kurt," Zola understood his concerned look. "Don't worry. I'm sure that isn't going to happen to your mom."

"Your mom is pregnant?" Madison asked.

"Yes. She's due in a month or so and she's been pretty down lately. Do you think I should worry or maybe mention something to my dad?"

"No, I think she's just feeling really blah just because that last month or two is really hard on a woman," Zola soothed. "She just needs you to be more sympathetic and understanding right now."

"Very well said, my dear," Mrs. Hendicott smiled at Zola. "And medicine has advanced dramatically since my day. Now there is therapy and medication to help if it does happen."

"You're sure?" Kurt asked.

"Yes. We can ask my mom if you want," Zola said.

"No..no that's all right. Thanks though. So," Kurt turned to Madison, eager to get the subject away from his mom, "go ahead and finish."

"So anyway, things got really bad after my grandfather, my mom's father died. He made up a new will after Zane was born and changed everything . My mom and dad began to argue a lot after that. I tried to listen, but they were pretty secretive about that in front of me.

"So when she got really bad, that's when my dad made her go to the doctor and sure enough that's what he felt was the problem. He prescribed some pills and some therapy and we all thought she was going to be all right. But she didn't get better. Things just seemed to get worse!"

"So your dad moved you guys here? To Fisherman's Haven?" Kurt asked.

"Yes. He thought it would be best if Mom's recovery was away from the city and away from Zane. He didn't want her to be all alone so I had to come. I don't know why he chose this place and I don't like it. I don't like the house. I don't like this town. I don't like anything or anyone here but Zola!" Madison cried again.

"So what don't you like about the house? I mean, the people here aren't all that bad, you just have to give them a chance, you know? But why the house?" Willie asked.

"It's creepy. It's like there's always someone watching, staring. It's like there's eyes on you all the time no matter what you are doing. And there's strange noises all the time. We only live in the one wing of the house and the other wing is blocked off, but there's strange noises all the time. The lights flicker off and on all the time. When I'm watching TV or listening to my stereo. The power dims and...it's just horrible! I don't think I've slept a whole night since we moved there!"

"How is your mom?" Willie asked.

"Oh! Don't even get me started on her!" Madison cried.

"Well, you have to tell us, you know," Kurt prodded.

"It's all right, Madison," Mrs. Hendicott soothed. Madison dabbed at her eyes with the tissue.

"She's worse! She says she hears things, people calling to her, she hears Zane crying in the night and then she hears furniture moving and now...lately...she...Oh! How can I tell them, Zola?" She burst out crying and pulled six tissues out of the box to cover her face.

"She says she is seeing ghosts," Zola said softly.

"Oh dear!" Mrs. Hendicott exclaimed.

"Yes," Zola began, "we were just there today and saw..."

"Ghosts, huh?" Willie's eyebrows arched cutting Zola off. His gaze locked with Kurt's. "Well, we're no ghost hunters, but we can certainly check some things out for you now that we know! I bet if we go through the house inch by inch, including the closed up wing, we'll find answers for those problems."

"Sure," Kurt smiled. "That banging is probably a window shutter or door with a broken hinge. That whispering is probably the wind coming through cracks in broken windows. Most of that stuff is explainable. What do you think, Zola?"

"You know what I think, Kurt. Just from the things Madison has told me and what happened to us today, I believe something is wrong there. I think we should investigate," Zola replied softly.

"We? What's this *we* thing?" Willie asked.

"Yes, *we*. Madison is my friend and I convinced her to seek your help. You do not think that I am going to sit back while you investigate the very thing that excites me! Not on your life!" Zola exclaimed.

"She's right!" Madison spoke up. "If you boys agree to help then you have to include Zola and me in this whole thing.

It's my house after all, and we wouldn't be here if Zola hadn't insisted that you guys were so great at finding things out."

"Well, I guess we could check a few things out," Willie agreed.

"What! Are you nuts!" Kurt cried. "Look what happened when we checked out the staircase?"

"What happened on the staircase?" Mrs. Hendicott asked.

"Nothing. Well, something. Well, we went through this door that was supposed to be locked, and we went through the door and there was this staircase and then the door slammed shut on us and then we saw this misty thing , but I think it was just our breath cause it was so cold in there and then the door opened," Kurt blurted out in one long breath.

"I see." Mrs. Hendicott had a peculiar look on her face.

"I think we can do this, Kurt. It shouldn't take too long. Madison can get us into the house again and now that we know the basic layout of everything, we can check out the rooms everywhere and at least see what we can see."

"Oh thank you! Thank you so much!" Madison threw her arms around Willie and hugged him. Willie's face turned twenty shades of red, but he didn't pull away!

"You know," Madison said when she finally did let Willie go, "I'm so glad I listened to Zola. I'm so sorry for acting the way I did to you guys. Well….to everyone I guess. But I was so afraid that everyone would find out what is going on….I was so ashamed about all the things my mom was saying about voices and ghosts. But now that I've talked to you all, I can see that I shouldn't be ashamed of her. I should try to help her and get down to the root of the problem. She never used to be this way. And now that I think about it, she must be so much more scared than I am! And…I love her."

"I might know a few things about that house," Mrs. Hendicott said. "I know that it is said to be haunted and that Madison and her mother are not dreaming, hallucinating or making anything up."

"Really?" Kurt, Willie, Madison and Zola said all together.

"Really," Mrs. Hendicott smiled. "I started thinking after you boys were here that night with Mai Su, bless her soul. She still comes by to check on the cats and see how things are going. She was here when Missy was brought back."

"Oh gee, we're really sorry," Willie slapped his forehead. "We should have come by."

"It's all right, I know you boys are busy. And Mai Su is such a help. She is a little abrupt and straightforward about things!" Mrs. Hendicott laughed. "She was telling me of that bear and how scared to death everyone was, and how those men shot at you and the bullet went right through your backpack and how brave you were!"

"Really?" Kurt blushed. "She said all that?"

"She is such a treasure."

"Speaking of. So tell us about this haunted house," Willie rolled his eyes at Kurt.

"Oh yeah, what about it?" Kurt grinned.

"I don't know much but I do remember that it has been unoccupied for more than fifty years. Oh, there has been an occasional renter but they never stay long. Same story, ghosts and noises. Scares the wits out of everyone and they just leave."

"So who owns the house?" Kurt asked.

"I'm not sure. I remember Grandfather speaking of it to Horace. It was built more than three hundred years ago, much the same as my old Victorian. There have been generations of the same family that lived there until the ghosts and noises drove him insane. He locked the place up and moved out!" she exclaimed.

"So, what's his name and where is he now?" Zola asked.

"It was something like Poleman… Portman… Pokeman or something and I'm not sure where he is." Everyone laughed. "What's so funny?"

"It's just that Pokeman was the name of a game years ago," Willie told her,

"Oh." And Mrs. Hendicott laughed, too.

"So how do we find out?" Willie asked.

"What would a true detective do?" Mrs. Hendicott peered at Willie over her glasses.

"Well…ah…"

"Search a paper trail," Zola said.

"Exactly!" beamed Mrs. Hendicott. "The historical society would have Towering Pines listed because it is so old. It would have the owners' names. From there you could follow that up at the…"

"Courthouse in Old Brunswicktown where the land transfers would have to be made at the county seat," Kurt said. "I know that because we had to go there when my dad bought our house. But how do we get there?"

"Richard," Madison said matter-of-factly.

"Oh, right. From there, we could check out the…." Willie waved his arms searching for help.

"Churches!" Mrs. Hendicott suggested.

"Churches?" The four echoed.

"Of course. Back in those days the church was the center of the town. All births, deaths, marriages, baptisms, you name it would have been written down in the church books."

"Mrs. Hendicott! You are a genius! See!" Willie nudged Madison on the shoulder. "I told you she would be a great help!"

"It was my idea," Kurt cried.

"I'm glad," Madison said. "Now we have a place to start. I…I just don't know how to thank you all for helping me."

"It's all right, my dear. Sometimes the solution to a problem is just a friend away. More chocolate anyone?"

Chapter Six

"We'd love to, Mrs. Hendicott," Willie said, standing up and stretching, "but I think we're going to head back to Madison's house and take another look around."

"We are?" Kurt asked echoed by Zola and Madison.

"Yes, we are, unless nobody else wants to get started on this right away. I guess we could wait until next weekend, but then..."

"All right, all right already," Kurt laughed and turned to the girls. "It's a time thing. The only time we actually have to investigate during school is on the weekends. We'll have to make arrangements to get to Old Brunswicktown sometime after school because that deeds office closes promptly at five."

"We can go on Wednesday," Madison said. "Agnes usually goes there on Wednesdays to do shopping and Richard can drop us off at the deeds office then take care of Agnes."

"Oh, a...can we trust her to keep this quiet? We don't want anyone knowing we are nosing around there," Willie said.

"She's all right. She's been with us since my mom was a baby for goodness sakes. Besides, if we tell our folks we are looking up stuff for a school project there won't be any issues, will there?" Madison suggested.

"Good idea! Hey you're pretty good at this!" Willie cried. "So, let's get going. Thanks Mrs. Hendicott for the chocolate and all the information."

"You are very welcome. Stop by and let me know how things are progressing!" She called to them and they waved to her from the sidewalk. They piled into the Chrysler and Richard once more started towards Towering Pines Manor. Nobody said a peep all the way because they didn't want to rouse Richard's suspicions.

It was nearly half past four when they turned onto the long twisting drive up to the Manor. Dusk settled early and the large pines blocked out any remainder of light from the final minutes of the winter day. The road had been cleared of its light dusting of snow and gleamed black beneath the cars headlights. Snow banks and drifts in the ditches looked like swirls over the uneven terrain. Kurt was staring out the window when a movement between the trees caught his attention. He jerked his head so hard he slammed it into the glass.

"What's with you?" everyone laughed.

"Nothing, just dozing I guess. That smarted!" He rubbed his forehead.

"Next time we'll let you sit in the middle," Zola said.

"No problem as long as it's between you girls!" he laughed.

"Don't be a poop head," Madison scowled.

"And don't start that scowling crap again," Kurt retorted back. Just because they had agreed to give Madison a second chance, he wasn't quite ready to forgive everything.

"I'm sorry," Madison said much to Kurt's surprise. "It's just that the closer I get to that place the more scared and angry I get. Sorry. I'll work on that."

Richard parked the Chrysler and jumped out to open the back door. Kurt, Willie, Zola and Madison were just starting for the stairs when a blood curdling scream reverberated through the cold night air followed by another and another.

"*MOM!*" Madison screamed. She threw open the door and raced for the stairs with Kurt, Willie and Zola right behind her. Richard pulled the front door shut and ran into Agnes, who came quickly from the sitting room, a dust rag dangling from her pocket.

"What is it?" she cried.

"Mrs. Demming!" Richard bolted up the stairs.

Madison was the first one through the door and the shock stopped her dead in her tracks. Kurt and Willie were so close behind her they slammed into her and thrust her into the room. She stumbled to the floor unable to catch her footing. Zola ran to her and helped her up. There, in the middle of the bed jumping blindly back and forth, pulling at her hair was Rozlin Demming shouting at the top of her lungs. Nurse Winthrop burst through, shoving Kurt and Willie to the side. She scurried back and forth along the bed trying to grab hold of the screaming woman.

"Oh please, Zola, help me stop her before she hurts herself!" Madison cried. She joined Nurse Winthrop at the bed.

"He's there! A man in my room! He was just there!" Mrs. Demming screamed and pointed towards the sitting room door.

"I'll get it!" Kurt ran towards where she was pointing, Willie at his heels. They pushed the door open and ran inside. The room was dark and Willie fumbled for the light switch. When he finally found it, they also found that the room was completely empty. They searched behind the chairs and the settee, as well as beneath the tables. They went back into the bedroom with a shrug. "There's nobody there now," Willie said.

"I saw him!" Mrs. Demming shouted. "I saw him when I woke up. I…I was lying down…resting…you see…and when I opened my eyes, he was there. Just standing there. Just standing there staring at me! He was dressed all in black and I couldn't see his face!" She finally allowed Nurse Winthrop to take her arm and pull her to sit on the bed. Madison put her arm around her shaking shoulders and smoothed the brown tendrils of hair back from her forehead.

"Are you sure, Mom? Are you sure you weren't just dreaming or something?"

"Oh Maddie, how can you ask me that? I am so frightened! Of course I'm sure! He was there. He was there staring at me. I want you to call the police!"

"Mrs. Demming, do you really think that is necessary?" Nurse Winthrop asked. She was already reaching for a sedative.

"No!" Madison put her hand on the nurse's arm. "You will not give her anything! This is almost broad daylight and if she saw someone in her room, then she saw someone in her room. Right, Mom?"

"Yes! Oh Maddie ,yes!" Mrs. Demming screamed. "Call the police or I'll not get a moments rest! Call them at once!"

"I'll call," Kurt said. "I'll just go use the phone downstairs."

"I'm coming…. with you," Willie said. He'd been looking around the room searching for a possible hiding spot that they'd overlooked. He was shocked when his eyes came to rest on a photo perched on Mrs. Demming's nightstand. He did a double take then, brushed past Richard in the doorway and followed Kurt out.

Agnes met them at the foot of the stairs. She was just setting the phone back on its cradle, her face anxious. "I heard her all the way from here. I've already called the police. They should be here any minute. Is Mrs. Demming all right? Shall I go up?"

"Yes. She's pretty frightened that's for sure. But Madison is there with her and so is that nurse. She'll be all right," Kurt answered. "We'll wait here and show the police up once they get here."

"I'm going to make her some hot tea," Agnes said and disappeared into the kitchen.

"Hey!" Kurt looked at Willie. "What was that weird look back in her bedroom?"

"Did you see the photo on her nightstand?"

"No, what about it?" Kurt asked.

"I....geez Kurt, I think it was Madison's mom and my mom, you know, back when they were younger."

"No!"

"I think so. Well, she was pretty skinny then and had really long hair and they were dressed in these silvery dresses and high heels and had tons of make-up on."

"But it could have been someone else, right? I mean, your mom and Madison's mom?" Kurt frowned. "How weird is that?"

"I know! I don't know what to make of that....Oh here's the police. Probably your dad."

Kurt opened the door before the knock. Sheriff Brandon stepped back in surprise. "Kurt? What are you doing here?"

"Come in, Dad. We were hanging out with Zola Dostoevsky and Madison Demming, that's who lives here, and just as we got here we heard this awful screaming coming from Mrs. Demming upstairs. She said there was someone in her room."

"An intruder?" Sheriff Brandon asked. He quickly followed the boys inside.

"Yes. But Dad, nobody here believes her because I guess she's been having some problems, (here Kurt pointed to his head) and she's on some heavy duty medication. They all think she was dreaming that it happened."

"All right, but I can tell by the tone of your voice that you don't agree with them?" he asked.

"No, I don't. Sorry Willie, but I never had a chance to tell you. When we were driving up here a few minutes ago, I thought I saw shadows running through the trees. It could have been animals or something, but I don't think so."

"Cliff," Brandon turned to his deputy, "take a look around outside then check around down here. I'll go up and get the statement."

"Gotcha!" Clifford Calhoun nodded and pulled the flashlight from his belt.

[55]

"Come on boys. Let's go see what's up." They started for the stairs. "SO! You boys are hanging around with girls?"

"*NO!*" They both shouted together.

"So Madison and Zola are not girls?" Brandon asked.

"Well, yes, they are, but it's not like that, Dad," Kurt said.

"Not at all like that, Mr. B," Willie echoed.

"Course not, course not."

They walked into Rozlin Demming's bedroom and any misgivings that her story was made up quickly vanished. She sat in the middle of the bed, her quilts pulled up tight around her, her body still shaking. Her long brown hair was matted and disheveled. Her large brown eyes were wide with fright and darted around the room continuously. She jumped when Kurt and Willie pushed past Richard and entered with Sheriff Brandon.

"Oh my God!" she cried with relief. "It's about time! He was there!" She pointed again towards the sitting room door. "He was there when I opened my eyes. I couldn't see his face. It was hidden. He was dressed all in black and.....he was there!"

"Mom, calm down. He's going to check, okay?" Madison put her arm around her mother's shaking shoulders.

"Mrs. Demming? I'm Sheriff Robert Brandon."

"Your dad?" mouthed Madison. Kurt nodded and shrugged.

... "and I will just need you to calm down and let's go over it one more time, slowly. About what time did you wake up and see this intruder?"

"About a half hour ago...no...no maybe more by now."

"And did anyone else see him?"

"No! I...at first I thought I was dreaming, so I blinked a couple of times, but he was still there and then he moved and then I just started screaming!"

"And you're sure it was a man?"

"I...I think so. But he was dressed in black with a hat on and it was dark in here......but...please you must believe me!"

She cried when she saw the look on everyone's face. "I did see someone!"

"And which way did he run when he disappeared?"

"There! Into the sitting room!" Mrs. Demming pointed again.

"Did anyone check that room?"

"We did, Dad. We checked everywhere and there was no one in there," Kurt answered.

Sheriff Brandon arched his eyebrows. "Go back and check again. Check for a hidden door or trap in the floor. Check everywhere again!"

"Okay." Kurt and Willie went back into the sitting room and this time they knocked on all the walls and practically tore down the drapes. Behind a large tapestry they found another door that exited into the hall. They returned with chins on their chest. "There's another door, Dad. It goes into the hall. But if whoever it was ran through that door, we would have seen him when we came up the stairs!" Kurt exclaimed.

"All right. Now then, Mrs. Demming, who was the first one to respond to your cries?"

"Why my nurse, Nurse Winthrop. She has a room right next to mine and she was the first one here."

"And did you see anyone or anything, Nurse Winthrop?" Sheriff Brandon turned to the heavy set woman patting Rozlin Demming's hand.

"No, Sheriff. By the time I came in the room and turned on the lights, there was no one here."

"Did you check?"

"No. My concern is my patient and she was standing in the middle of the bed screaming her head off and tearing her hair out. My first concern was to get her to come down from the bed and calm down. I have given her a sedative so you had better ask your questions before it fully takes effect."

"I told her not to!" Madison cried. "I told her to wait until you had time to question her, but she wouldn't wait!"

"I see." Sheriff Brandon turned his attention back to Rozlin Demming. Already she was having trouble keeping her eyes open and her head slumped back onto the pillow. "I think I have enough for now. I will keep you informed, Mrs. Demming."

"Thank you. Thank you very much. No thank you Agnes. I don't want any tea. Please show the sheriff out." Rozlin Demming gripped Madison's hand, "Don't go, Maddie. Stay for a few more minutes."

"I will, Mom," Madison said. "I'll stay as long as you want me to."

"Let's go boys. I'll take you home. You too, Zola. I'm sure your parents are wondering where you are."

"Thank you, sir," Zola said. She gave Madison a reassuring smile and turned to follow them out.

"Zola wait!" Madison called. "Please ask your parents if you can stay over! I'm so frightened! I really could use a good friend to stay with me tonight!"

"I will call and ask," Zola smiled at her.

"Dad," Kurt said stopping in the hall. "Take a look at this." He pointed to the wall. "That door to Mrs. Demming's sitting room is here but you can't tell because they have the panel looking like any other panel along the wall. And anyone doing a check of the room would certainly miss it like we did because it is hiding behind a large tapestry hanging on the wall on the other side!"

"Yeah, so if she really did see someone in there, we could have already gone past this into her room, then they could have sneaked out and no one would have seen them," Willie added.

"And you know what else?" Kurt scratched his head. "Now that I think of it, wasn't Madison the first one in the room?"

"You're right!" Willie cried. "And we were right behind her. It wasn't until then that the nurse came in. I remember now because she shoved between us to get to Mrs. Demming!"

"So that means she lied!" Kurt cried.

"She didn't actually lie, Kurt. She didn't say at all whether she was the first one in. Mrs. Demming said that," Sheriff Brandon corrected him.

"So what! Lied by omission! Isn't that just as much of a lie as if she said it herself?" Willie asked.

"Look, Dad, another thing. I know the driver Richard was with us because he dropped us off at the door when the screaming started. Then he rushed up here with the rest of us. But he seems to have disappeared because I don't see him anywhere."

"He could have gone to put the car away, Kurt. But I am sure Deputy Calhoun will have seen to questioning him."

"Dad?"

"What is it, Kurt?" They finally continued down the stairs, but Kurt stopped once more. "Is it all right if we stay here tonight? I mean, Madison is just as scared as her mom and the only guy here is Richard, the driver. The others are old women and you know how they are. They don't understand how upset and scared Madison really is. It would really make her feel better if we stayed. And besides, it might help if they knew there was other help in the house. At least for tonight."

"Yeah! Can we?" Willie asked.

Zola met them on the stairs. "I've already telephoned my parents. They have given me permission to stay. Thank you for your offer, Sheriff Brandon." Zola smiled sweetly and returned to Madison.

"Geez, Dad! Can we stay?" Kurt pleaded. The boys followed Kurt's dad down the stairs.

"Yeah! They need us!" Willie said.

Sheriff Brandon, hesitated, his hand on the door knob. He searched the boy's faces. "I understand you boys want to help, but you see my dilemma here. Two young teens, spending the night with girls!"

"Geez, Dad, are you kidding?" Kurt shrank back.

"No I am not. I hope you boys keep our conversation of the birds and the bees well in mind here."

"Promise Mr. B. We are just going to stay and make sure things are all right, that's all!" Willie exclaimed, feeling embarrassed by the reminder.

"All right then. I will tell your mom, and Willie I will get in touch with your parents. You *call* if anything happens, got that?"

"We will, Dad, thanks. We'll go tell Madison we're staying." Kurt bounded back up the stairs, Willie at his side.

"Great idea!" Willie whispered excitedly.

"I know! Give us a chance to really look this place over, don't you think?"

"Sure was embarrassing wasn't it? I mean your dad saying that stuff. Didn't anyone tell him that nobody really likes Madison Demming!" Willie whispered.

"Well, nobody but you," Kurt smirked.

"Oh man!" Willie punched Kurt in the arm.

Chapter Seven

Madison nearly jumped out of her skin when she heard the tap and Willie peeked his head inside. "Is all right if we come in?" he whispered.

"Oh doggonit! You scared the wits out of me!" Madison hissed. "Come in. My mom's sleeping. Nurse Winthrop gave her a really strong sedative. She makes me so mad! I explicitly told her not to. I hate when she gives that stuff to my mom. She doesn't even give her a chance to be a normal person anymore."

"She looks like she's sleeping pretty soundly, Madison," Zola whispered. "I think it's what she needs right now."

"Maybe. After all it is the only time she doesn't have those awful nightmares."

"How are you doing?" Kurt asked.

"I'm okay I guess. Still frightened, though."

"We figured that. That's why we convinced my dad to let us stay here for the night," he added.

"Really? Oh, I am so glad! Zola is staying too so at least I won't be alone and not so scared." Madison heaved a sigh of relief. She glanced to her mom who had shifted in her sleep. The hand that had been gripping Madison's relaxed and let go.

"I think she just sank into that deep sleep those shots promise."

"Good. Is there somewhere we can go and talk?" Willie asked.

"Sure. Let's go to my room. It's just down the hall." Madison tucked the blankets around her mom, gave her a light kiss on the forehead and motioned for Kurt, Zola and Willie to follow. She closed the door with a soft click. "Come on, I'm just right here. With all the stuff going on in this house I decided to have my room close to Mom's so we could comfort each other if we needed to."

Madison led them into a room that was bigger than Willie's and Kurt's rooms put together. Painted in shades of mauve and maroon, it had heavy maroon drapes covering the large windows that spanned the back of her room. A paisley wall paper print was midway from the wall to the ceiling and matched the large area rug that covered most of the hardwood floor.

A large double bed was to their left. There was a circular nightstand draped with a paisley print cloth on either side of the bed. Beneath the windows were built in bookcases and in between were window seats tucked into neat little alcoves. Along the wall to their right were several large wardrobes. One stood open, spilling with unfolded and unhung clothes. Madison walked over to the wardrobe and stuffed everything inside. She latched the doors shut and leaning against them, turned to the boys with an apologetic shrug.

"So what did you want to talk about?"

"Well, there's tons of things we want to ask," Willie began. He walked to one of the window seats and peered out between the drapes. It was nearly a moonless night, just a sliver of deep yellow penetrated the clouds that scudded through the dark sky. Below nothing was stirring but the heavy snow laden branches of the pines softly soughing in the wind. "First off, I guess we should start with the hired help. How long has this Richard character been with you?"

"He's been my driver for over ten years. He came with us from Boston."

"Ten years! He doesn't look old enough for that!" Kurt cried.

"Well, he's over thirty from what I know. He's pretty quiet and I don't think Richard is his real name. Dad just started calling him that because he couldn't pronounce his real name. He's from somewhere in the Ukraine. He managed to escape over here and with help from my dad he got his entire family out before all that fighting got really bad. He gives them most of his earnings. I don't think we have to worry about him at all. He's really loyal and grateful to my dad."

"Oh, okay. Then what about this Agnes woman?"

"Good grief! You don't suspect Agnes of anything? She was my mother's housekeeper when my mom was just a little girl. She loves my mom and dotes on her like she was her own. She has a heart of gold and wouldn't hurt a fly, although I think if anyone tried to hurt my mom she might resort to madness." Madison sat on her bed.

"And then there's Nurse Winthrop," Madison continued. "I don't know much about her because she was hired by my dad when we moved here. She's supposed to be one of those specialists that deals with women after.....well with women who have breakdowns after they have a child."

"So she's only been with you guys maybe the month or so you've lived here?" Kurt asked taking a seat in the second window seat.

"Yes. My dad says she has complete control and authorization regarding Mom's well-being and medical care, and we're not to interfere. What I do know is that Agnes doesn't like her."

"I wonder why?" Willie asked.

"You've just met the woman! What *is* there to like? She's bossy. *She* tells Agnes *when* my mom eats. *She* tells Agnes *what* my mom eats. *She* tells Agnes *when* my mom must rest or is allowed visitors. Actually, she's just so annoying."

"I should say so," Willie peered out the window again.

"Are you looking for something?" Zola asked.

"No...no...just thinking is all," Willie answered. "And what about the cooking staff?"

"Oh, that is Shelby Matterly. She's from town, a local girl. She seems to be pretty nice."

"We know Shelby, Kurt," Willie said. "Her folks have the farm next to old man Barnaby and Shelby used to work part time cooking at that truck stop."

"Oh sure. She is really nice. Wouldn't hurt a fly."

"So that leaves us with only the nurse with a sketchy background. I wonder how we can find out more about her," Willie mused.

"I could ask my dad," Madison suggested. "He said he was going to be here in the morning."

"He told you that?" Kurt asked. "You called him?"

"No, Agnes called him and told him it was an emergency. He said he would get here right away. Things'll be all right once he gets here." Madison banked the pillows and leaned against the headboard of the bed. "Wow! I can't believe how tired I am. Look, I should show you two where you can sleep. There's a room two doors down with two beds in it. You can crash there."

"Don't bother getting up," Kurt put his hand to stop her. "We can find it. By the way, do you have any flashlights around?"

"Do I have flashlights? Do I have flashlights!" Madison jumped up and reached beneath her bed. Three flashlights. She pulled open the lid on the box on her night table. Two flashlights. She ran to her wardrobe and pulled open the big drawer beneath the doors. Five flashlights there. She ran to the window seat that Kurt had vacated and lifted the seat. Four more flashlights there.

"Geez!" Willie exclaimed. "Fanatic much!"

"I don't care. There's so much weird stuff happening in this house that I went and bought every flashlight in the store. I'm not going to get caught in the dark in this place!"

"Well, we don't want *all* of them, just a couple." Kurt reached for two with large heads. "These'll do just fine."

"What are you two planning to do?" Zola asked.

"Oh, nothing. We just wanted to have a look around downstairs once more. After all that fiasco of a tour you gave us was…well…a fiasco." Willie grabbed one of the lights and tucked it into his back pocket.

"Then I'm coming," Madison said matter of factly.

"Me too," Zola rose from the bed.

"Oh no you're not!" Kurt whirled on Madison. "You never know when to shut up! You always scream at everything! You don't know how to take orders and just listen to someone else. Always gotta be the boss with your snooty attitude. We can't have you interfering with what we want to do. We can't have everyone knowing that we are snooping. You are staying right here!"

"Well —— geez—that's not very nice!" Madison stepped back and glared at Kurt.

"Sorry, but it's true," Kurt retorted.

"If I promise…"

"No!" Both boys cried at once. Willie continued, "Tonight we check things out alone. You just stay here with Zola and if you want you can wait up for us. We'll check back in when we get done. All right?"

Madison looked from one stern face to another. "All right, all right already."

"Good. Let's go Kurt."

The boys ignored Madison standing there staring at them with her hands planted on her hips, that same snooty look on her face as before. They left, closing the door firmly behind them and stepped into the hall. The soft glow of the hall lamps gave them enough light to find their way back downstairs where Willie stopped at the front door and did an about face "What is the plan?" Kurt asked.

"I was thinking we'd start right here. Head down that hall there," Willie pointed to his immediate left, "and go all the way around checking everything as we go."

"Great idea." Kurt followed Willie. The hall was wide and had large potted plants along the wall that faced outside and a long hall bench with several hooks for coats and hats. Willie sidled up to the edge of the window and looked out. Kurt did the same. There was nothing moving outside, and they couldn't see past the   reflection of light on the snow. They moved on. At the end the hall turned to the right and they entered into the large kitchen. It smelled of disinfectant and the tiled floors glistened where the tiny pot lights beneath the counters spread round circles of diffused light over the kitchen. A swinging door led them into the dining room.

"So what do you make of all this?" Kurt finally asked breaking the silence.

"I don't know, Kurt. This whole situation has got me baffled, that's for sure."

"Well, at least now we know why Madison was such a snobby witch to everyone."

"Not to mention the bags and puffy eyes. She must be scared out of her wits," Willie whispered. "Look at this room, will you?"

"I know, hey? I guess we should have paid more attention when we ate the snack in here but I was so mad at Madison back then." Kurt looked around.

"I know, me too."

The dining room was a grand room of dark maple paneled walls and intricately carved chair rails. Two mullioned windows were to the right with large potted ferns on each side that swayed gently with the breath of air that seeped through the crack putty of the old windows. In the center of the room was a large table with six high-backed chairs, the table centerpiece a mastery of garland and winter flowers. They continued through the dining room that led them back into the foyer.

"We've gone around in a circle. That was easy." Willie looked around. "Come on. Let's check out the sitting room."

They pushed open the door to the sitting room. It was dark inside and the faint light from the hall cast shadows into the far corners. Small tables, stuffed chairs, sofas and potted plants filled every nook and cranny of the room. There was a six foot tall fir tree decorated for Christmas with large glass bulbs and old fashioned tinsel hanging from its branches. The tinsel sparkled and fluttered in the disturbed air. Behind that was the patio door framed by a large set of windows on each side along the wall that faced the back of the house. The heavy drapes were now drawn against the cold and dark . The boys crossed the room. They edged around the tree, drew apart the heavy drapes and saw a veranda that resembled the entry with its large pillars and covered portico. In the summer it would have been a welcoming patio but now was covered with a thick blanket of snow. The boys stood in the shadows and stared out for quite some time. "What are we looking for?" Kurt finally broke the silence.

"I don't know. I got to thinking about what you told your dad. That you thought you saw someone in the woods when we were driving up."

"I didn't think I saw someone. There was someone. I know what an animal looks like when it is running and this was no animal, Willie. It was a human being."

"I believe you, especially after what happened tonight."

"So what are you thinking?"

"I'm thinking that there are no ghosts here at all. I'm thinking that someone is sneaking in and out of here and trying to scare Madison's mom half to death."

"Why would anyone want to do that?" Kurt drew back in surprise.

"I don't know yet."

"Why here?"

"Maybe it started when they lived in Boston. Didn't Madison say her mom started getting weird back there?"

"Yes, she did."

"So, maybe they just kept it up once she and Madison moved down here?"

"But who would do such a thing and why?"

"I don't know. But I think it has to do with that money from the grandfather who changed his will at the last minute," Willie said. "It doesn't look like whoever is coming in is using these doors. There are no tracks in the snow."

"It's a good theory to start with," Kurt admitted. "Come on. There's still a lot to look at." They let the drapes fall back into place. The room held an eerie silence and large shadows seemed to quiver strangely when they ran their flashlights into the deep recesses of the corners where the hall light did not reach. Back in the hall they eyed the door that led into the unused wing that Madison said was locked. Willie tugged on the handle. Sure enough, it was locked. "Come on, the solarium."

The solarium was a huge room that spanned the front of the house to the right of the entry door. It opened up into a ten foot wide space that extended nearly twenty feet in length, taking it to the far corner of the original house. The floor was black and white marble. A solid wall of oak framed windows comprised the front wall. Pots of plants stood everywhere with hanging plants suspended from hooks along the way. In the center was a water fountain. The gentle trickling of water from the spout of the cupid's arrow seemed to echo in the eerie silence of the sleeping house. Off to one corner was a cushioned lounge chair, a small glass topped table and several iron chairs.

"Doesn't look like much can go on in here," Kurt whispered. "Doesn't it seem odd that both times we came here we never noticed all these windows?"

"We had other things on our minds," Willie said. He began checking behind several large plants while Kurt made his way to the far end of the room. He leaned against the wall for balance. The wall wavered beneath his fist.

"Hey, Willie, come here!"

"What! What do you got there?" Willie quickly ran over.

"There's another door here. It's hard to tell because it's blocked by these plants but look at this!" Kurt cried out and bent down pinning the flashlight beam to the floor.

"Just what we figured!" Willie bent down and they both played their flashlights to the floor. "Scratch marks! Looks like someone moved these pots to get at this door because this… door… opens." He pushed on the blind door and it opened silently inward "And there we are! Another staircase!"

"Come on!" Kurt whispered taking the lead. Several steps up, he pointed. "Look there! Shoe prints!" Willie nodded. He closed the door behind him and they followed the steps, making sure they didn't disturb the prints just in case they needed them for evidence later. The staircase went up steeply then turned to the left. Here they came face to face with another door. Kurt turned the handle. It gave no resistance and a few seconds later, Kurt and Willie were standing in a familiar hall.

"So this is where that door leads to!" Willie exclaimed.

"Zola wanted to try these stairs. If we'd have listened to her in the first place, we would have found that secret entrance from the solarium and told my dad about it."

"Then he would have taken over everything and we would be out of the picture," Willie added.

"Did that ever stop us before?" Kurt grinned.

"Course not. Let's check this out. As long as we don't have those squealing girls, we can take our time."

Chapter Eight

They closed the door behind them and stood silently in the same hall that they'd been in earlier that day. Just ahead was the door partially hidden in the recessed alcove that led to the upper staircase where the mist had been seen. Kurt shuddered. "You hear that?"

"Yeah, what do you think it is?"

"Not sure. Sounded like a thump, like something falling or something banging into something." Kurt played the flashlight around.

"It stopped," Willie said.

"I'll bet if we can get up into that room up there," Kurt pointed his light towards the stairs, "we would find that there's a loose board or a shutter banging in the wind."

"Probably. Sure put a crimp in all that mumbo jumbo that Zola says about ghosts and spirits, wouldn't it?"

"Hey! That's not fair. She's only trying to help!"

"Help? By scaring the wits out of everyone? Isn't Madison freaked enough?"

"Well, she ….." Kurt began, but Willie cut him off.

"Let's check out these rooms while we're here."

Kurt nodded and let the matter drop. There wasn't any point in beginning an argument with Willie. Especially about a girl. They had agreed a long time ago that nothing, not even a girl, not *especially* a girl, would ever come between their friendship or their goals in life.

They turned right and retraced their steps from earlier that day. Straight up ahead was the door that, according to Madison, was supposed to be locked, but wasn't because they had been able to get in from that door earlier that day. They knew that one of the doors on their right had been looked into and was another sitting room. Off to their left was one large set of sliding doors that they had not particularly noticed their first time in as the doors much resembled the paneled wall. It was apparent to them now, when their lights caught the recessed brass handles in the wood , that it indeed was another room. They decided to check that out first. They slid the doors open where they disappeared into the wall. "Hey that is so cool!" Kurt cried.

"I know, don't you just love these old houses? They have so much personality, something new houses today don't have." Willie walked inside.

"Personality? Where did that come from?"

"Oh I don't know. I was just thinking about Mrs. Hendicott's house. Horace's treasure room was specially built to house all those books and artifacts. Back hundreds of years ago builders did cool stuff like that. Now you look at new houses and they are like prefab, all the same, slapped on tiling, slapped up drywall and there's nothing there to give them character, you know?"

"I don't know if you're saying it right, but I do know what you mean. This room is so awesome! It's the library! Look at all the shelves! I bet they're filled with books. Too bad there's dust covers on everything. I'll bet there's some really cool stuff on these shelves."

The room was huge. Bookshelves lined the walls from floor to ceiling and even the recessed window seats had shelves built into the walls surrounding them. Heavy drapes were closed against the outside and the room was dark as pitch. There was a sofa and several chairs, a center table and small round tables around the room all covered in dust cloths. Books were stacked in piles along the existing cases, some knocked over and covered with dust where they had fallen. It smelled of old books, old leather and cigars.

"Over here, Kurt look at this!" Willie had zigzagged through the maze of stacked books on the floor and was now at the desk that was near a large fireplace.

Kurt crossed to where Willie stood staring down at something. "A book? Wow look at that! It's made of leather and thick as nails!" He reached for the cover. Willie pulled his hand back.

"Don't you think it's really odd that everything in this room is covered in dust clothes but this desk and this book."

"I didn't think much of anything. There wasn't any time, but now that you mention it, I guess it is odd."

"What's that?" Willie's head shot up, ears perked.

"What?" Kurt looked around.

"That bumping noise again."

"I didn't hear anything," Kurt said.

"Must be spooks. Anyway, don't you think that's odd?"

"Well sure. It means that someone was in here and looking at this book," Kurt added.

"Maybe."

"Maybe? What do you mean maybe? What else could it be?"

"Then why leave it uncovered? Why not cover everything back up again so no one would ever know," Willie reasoned.

"For one thing, I think whoever it was that was in here looking through that book didn't expect that anyone would be coming around investigating anything."

"Well that's certainly true. But why would someone be in here in the first place?"

"I don't know. It could have been someone from a long time ago. It could be someone who lives in the house now. It could be the guy we're trying to find that's doing the haunting of Mrs. Demming. I don't know!" Kurt cried.

"Geez, don't get all freaky on me. It's bad enough the girls do that. There has to be some reason why this is uncovered. It can't be nothing."

"Nothing...schmothing! Open the darn thing," Kurt cried.

Willie cast Kurt an angry look but finally eased the heavy leather cover of the book open. The binding creaked and groaned as the book fought to open. "Sudbury," Kurt read.

"Sudbury— must be like a family tree book," Willie repeated the name. He turned back the next several pages before he came to some names. "Look at this picture!"

"Wow! That's like one of those pictures they used to take with those big standup cameras that they had to put a cover on the lens, know what I mean! Look at that! It's so cool!"

"Yeah. It was taken on a sunny day and everything looks so new. Check out the front of the house, Kurt. The solarium isn't there in this picture."

"You're right. It must have been added later. But there are lots of windows there and a couple of doors. I wonder where they led to."

"So look here," Willie turned the page. "It looks like a history of the people that lived here. Lucky we found this because we would have been searching for Towering Pines Manor at the deeds office when it really was originally called Sudbury House."

"It says here, Sudbury House, built 1645 by Jacob Sudbury. Jacob Sudbury born 1615 died 1698. Ruth Sudbury born 1655, died 1683. Matthew Sudbury born of Jacob and Ruth Sudbury, February 1680. Wow that means Ruth the mother died when Matthew was only three years old."

"Poor kid. Turn the page. Look there, a picture of Jacob and Ruth when they got married." Kurt whistled. "Look at those two, hey? Black suits with white collars like Puritans or something."

"They look like that old painting of that farmer and his wife, remember? The one with the hay fork?" Willie laughed.

"Actually with those pointed noses and glued back hair styles they look like something out of Shakespeare's plays." Kurt shivered. "Ewwe! Reminds me of English class, flip the page. See there. It's a picture of two more. Hard to read, I think it says.....yeah there it is, Matthew Sudbury born 1680, died 1752. Clara Judson Sudbury born 1710, died 1728. Caleb Jacob Sudbury born to Matthew and Clara Sudbury June 1728. This one means his mom must have died in childbirth. Geez the women in this family sure don't have any longevity do they."

"It sure is looking that way. Here," Willie flipped the page again. "This one is written in darker ink. What's that?" He spun around and moved the flashlight back and forth across the room.

"What did you hear?"

"I keep hearing those thumping sounds. Driving me nuts! Wish I could pinpoint where they are coming from."

"Probably upstairs. Loose board like I said. Who's the freaked out one now?" The grin fell from Kurt's face when he saw the anger flare in Willie's eyes. "Come on. Keep reading. I didn't hear a thing. This page says Caleb Sudbury born 1728, died 1820. Wow! He sure got to be an old man!" Kurt avoided Willie's stare and continued reading. "Mary Clair Jones Sudbury born 1760, died 1793. Geez, another wife that died young. But at least they had lots of kids."

"Read on, none of them lived. Here's one for Elizabeth Ann Sudbury born 1785, died 1785. Bartholomew James Sudbury born 1786, died 1788. Mary Rose Sudbury born 1787, died 1789. Blaine John Sudbury born 1788, died 1790. Matthias Silvan Sudbury born 1790 , no date for the death. Well, at least one of their kids survived."

"Sure, but like I said, it isn't looking too good for the women in this family," Kurt said.

"All right, where does that leave us. We got up to 1881 when Matthias dies. Flip the page, Kurt," Willie said. "Ah, here it is. Matthias Silvan Sudbury born 1790, died 1881 married Lorraine Dobson Sudbury born 1810, died 1826."

"Geez! She was only sixteen! You think she died on her wedding night?"

"Look here," Willie continued. "Another Matthias Sudbury married Elizabeth Ann Cleary in 1827. Elizabeth Ann Cleary Sudbury, born 1805, died 1830. Then Matthias Sudbury married Abigail Newton 1835. Abigail Newton Sudbury born 1820, dies 1840. Are you getting the feeling that I'm getting?"

"What's that?" Kurt asked.

"Look at this. Matthias Sudbury marries three women. Each one of them is only like fifteen or sixteen years old. Each one of them dies almost right away. Don't you find that strange?"

"Sure is. Like he was marrying them and killing them off until he got one he really wanted. Maybe it was that dowry thing."

"Dowry?" Willie stared at him not understanding.

"You know back in the day when a man married a woman, the woman's parents had to give her a dowry like money or land. Maybe that's what old Matthias was all about. Getting their money and their land and then bumping them off. There's nothing here that tells us how the Sudbury's managed to be so influential and rich is there?"

"No.....you could be right. But then that would make him a murderer!"

"Maybe it runs in the family. Keep reading. See if there's any more."

"Okay. So Matthias and Abigail had a son named Faraday...Faraday? What a strange name. A son Faraday born 1835, died 1905."

Kurt turned the page. "Okay so here is Faraday with his wife Margaret born 1850, died 1891. They had a daughter Mary Elizabeth born 1890 and there is no entry for a death."

"That seems strange. It's not like she'd still be living would she?" Kurt frowned.

"Turn the page. What else does it say?" Willie asked. "There it is. Looks like the guy, what does it say? August James Polchet married Mary Elizabeth Sudbury in 1910 and had a son Tobias James Polchet. But he must not have loved her very much because he shredded her face right out of the picture!"

"What does it say for his life and death?" Kurt asked. "Here it is, August James Polchet born 1889, died 1952. Oh my God! We finally made it to a century we can understand!" Kurt cried.

"But then the book ends. There are no more entries and there are no pictures. We have nowhere else to go. If this Tobias James Polchet was the last surviving relative to the Jacob and Ruth Sudbury genealogy, where does that leave this house? Who owns it now? Where is he?"

"But we have a name to go on. We can check back on Tobias James Polchet at the court house and do like Mrs. Hendicott said and check the registers at the churches. That's a start," Kurt said.

"Doggone it! What *is* that thumping!" Willie whirled around quickly shooting his flashlight from corner to corner.

"Shhhh!" Kurt whispered. "I finally hear it!"

They stood still, their hands poised over the pages of the Sudbury book. Darkness seemed to close in around them and the thumping grew louder, drifting closer. It filled the entire room and had no beginning and no end. Kurt shivered. Pinpricks of fear raised the hairs on the back of his neck. Beside him Willie held his breath and his face paled as he leaned forward, straining to hear. Penetrating the thumping was the unmistakable sound of something dragging across the timbers overhead. A drag. Silence. A drag. With every nerve stiffened by fear, with every muscle tensed, both boys jerked back when an icy chill swept over them and a high pitched agonizing scream pierced their eardrums, then faded slowly into silence. Kurt and Willie stared at each other for just a second, then ran for the door. "The book! Get the book!" Willie shouted to Kurt behind him. "We're taking it with us!"

Kurt grabbed the book, tucked it under his arm and raced to catch up to Willie. He really didn't have to because Willie had stopped in the hall with his ear cocked to listen. Kurt slammed into him, shoving him against the wall.

"Sorry! Did you hear anything more?" Kurt looked around frantically.

"No! Just listen!" But the thumping had stopped. The screaming had subsided into nothing. The hall was bathed in darkness, the air electrified with fear. And then....

A soft moaning, barely audible, reached their ears, muffled and weak that turned to sobbing. Willie cocked his head. "Over there," he motioned towards the wood door that had slammed on them earlier that day.

"Who the heck would be up there?" Kurt mouthed.

"Come on." Willie inched cautiously forward step by slow step until they stood face to face with the old wooden door once more. It was unlocked earlier, and they had been able to get inside only to be trapped in the darkness for ten terrifying minutes. It was there that the mist had swept up the curving staircase, it was there that the thumping had come from, it was there the boys could hear the muffled sounds of a woman weeping.

Their eyes met. Fear met fear. Finally Kurt nodded and Willie gripped the handle, his hand shook when he wrapped his sweaty palms around it. His thumb pressed the latch and the releasing click thundered in the cold stillness of the hall. Willie's breath caught in his throat and Kurt nearly dropped the book. Then Willie pulled the door open quickly and thrust the beam of his flashlight upon the stairs.

A mist of fine white floated before them, up the stairs and around the turn, the sobbing following in its wake. The boys gulped. "Come on!" Willie gripped Kurt by the shoulder and together they crept up the stairs. Slowly, step by step they inched forward, the mist disappearing from view, the sobbing fading into the distance until they reached the curve. Goosebumps prickled their arms and their neck hairs bristled once more. Willie wiped the sweat from his palms. Kurt scrunched side by side with him, sweat sticking his shirt to his armpits. He swiped it from his forehead. The steps continued rising higher and higher, turning like the spiral steps of the old lighthouse, finally reaching the top. And there at the landing stood another door.

"We must be in that tower that we saw over the pines!" Kurt whispered. "Remember when we were driving up and we could see it? This must be it."

"Yeah," Willie's trembling hand reached for the handle on the door. A door of thick timbers braced with iron bars across the top, bottom and center, sealed shut with an old lock that looked just as shiny black and new as the first day it had locked away the secret that lay inside. Willie grabbed the lock and jerked it this way and that. It was not budging. "Look! There's no dust or anything up here. I think someone's been here, too." He finally stepped back and drew a deep breath.

"So how does that explain that....that...thing we saw on the stairs?"

"Don't know. But no dust has to mean it's a real person, not some ghost or spirit like Zola thinks."

"But it still doesn't explain…"

"We will, Kurt. Don't go getting all paranormal on me. Do you believe that sort of stuff?" Willie turned on Kurt and stared at him, pushing aside his own fears from moments ago.

"I…I don't know…I guess I do to some degree. I mean , if people have souls and the Bible tells us there are such things as angels and devils and stuff, why can't there be spirits? Isn't that sort of the same as a soul?"

"Oh brother! I can see we're going to have to quit hanging around Zola. She's starting to rub off on you."

"Yeah? You should talk. I saw your hand shaking when you reached for that handle."

"Was not!"

"Was too!"

"Was not!"

"Oh stop it! What difference does it make. Something weird is going on here and we have to find out what," Kurt said.

"And why," Willie added.

"Hey, let's head back and check on the girls. Doesn't look like we're going to break through that lock anyway. They're probably hiding under the bed with all the flashlights on after hearing that scream."

"I forgot all about them. Let's go," Willie said.

They retraced their steps and this time, the door at the bottom of the circular stairs was still open. They closed it quickly and leaned against the wall.

"Are we going to tell the girls about this?" Kurt asked.

"No. Not just yet anyway. They will freak for sure!" Willie said.

"That was the strangest thing *ever*!" Kurt wiped his face with the sleeve of his shirt.

"Were you really scared?" Willie asked.

"Sort of. Were you?"

"Sort of."

"Weird, right?"

"Yeah, weird. Come on. We'd better see how the girls are doing." They walked back through the hall, through the door that was *supposed* to be locked and found themselves back in the hall where just three doors down was Madison's room.

Willie tapped on the door and Madison thrust it open so fast they nearly tumbled inside. "You all right?" Willie asked.

"Yes!" she cried breathlessly. "We've been waiting here for you for eons! What's been going on? What did you find? Where did you go?"

"You mean you...you girls didn't hear that scream a while ago?" Kurt asked.

"No, I haven't heard a thing since you guys left."

"I didn't hear anything but I could feel something," Zola whispered from the bed.

"It's okay. Zola explained to me all about her special gift. I understand. We did go and check on my mom a couple of times and she's still sleeping. So I've been pacing here waiting for you two. What happened? What scream? What do you have there?" Madison finally noticed the book tucked beneath Kurt's arm.

Kurt had quite forgotten he had the book tucked there. He was hanging on to it so tightly that his fingers ached when he finally set the book down on the bed.

"It's a genealogy of who lived here. Come and take a look," Willie said. Everyone crowded around.

The Hidden Secret of Towering Pines Manor

Chapter Nine

They woke to a bright sunlight streaming in through the windows. Kurt rolled over and pried his eyes open. It was several moments before he remembered that they were in a bedroom at Madison's house and had finally turned out the lights around four in the morning. He rolled over once more and saw the small clock on the nightstand. He bolted out of the bed and shouted to Willie in the next bed, "Willie! Willie! Willie get up! Geez it's nine-thirty!"

"So what!" Willie groaned in his pillow.

"Madison's dad is supposed to be coming today. We'd better get out of here!" Kurt quickly pulled on his jeans and sweatshirt, then hastily pulled the quilts up over the bed.

"Oh man!" Willie bounded out of the bed. It was several minutes before he found his sneakers then flung the blankets over the pillows.

It was quiet in the hall, so they tip-toed downstairs. Just when they were reaching for their jackets, Madison came out of the solarium, her arm threaded around the elbow of a tall, dark-haired man.

"Hey you guys! Bout time you got up!" she cried excitedly. "This is my dad, Collin Demming. Isn't it great? He got here about an hour ago."

"Oh, hi, Mr. Demming. My name is Kurt, Kurt Brandon." He looked like a fool with one arm pushed into the sleeve of his jacket and the other struggling overhead to find the hole of the other.

"It is a pleasure to meet you, Kurt Brandon." Collin Demming shook Kurt's dangling hand.

"Ah, Willie McLeish, sir," Willie held out his hand.

Collin Demming seemed to look strangely at Willie, his expression one of sudden intense interest. He searched Willie's face, his hair, his eyes, the tall lankiness before his gaze rested on Willie's face once more. He seemed to come to with a start, reached out and gripped Willie's outstretched hand. "Pleasure to meet you, Willie McLeish. Madison tells me you were both very helpful to her and her mother. I am grateful to you both. But, as we have much to discuss, I am sure you won't mind if we do so in private?"

"Ah, no…no..not at all," Willie stuttered. "We were just leaving."

"Richard is waiting outside, he will take you home. Good day." Collin Demming turned, smiled at Madison then steered her towards the stairs and out of sight.

"Whew! Talk about dismissal!" Kurt tugged on his jacket. "Let's get out of here."

Zola was already waiting in the car. "Oh, you, too," Willie muttered getting in.

"Yes. He said if you both didn't come downstairs in like one more minute he would send Richard to get you. He sounded very displeased. Mr. Demming is not a very nice person," Zola said.

"I guess not." Kurt slammed the door. "Home, Richard."

Richard had them home in ten minutes and Kurt got out at Willie's. They entered the house and could smell coffee brewing. "Mom? Dad?" Willie called out. "Man, they must be at church. They are going to be so mad that we missed."

"Well, it was for a good cause. I am sure my dad explained everything to them. Hey look here, fresh pot of coffee, some waffles warming in the oven and o.j. on the table. Your mom must have known we would be back soon. Wonder if I should call my mom." Kurt grabbed a plate and piled it with waffles.

"Probably at church, too," Willie stuffed half a waffle in his mouth on his way to the frig for the milk.

"So, what do you think is our next move?" Kurt reached for the syrup. He let the book fall from beneath his jacket onto the counter.

"Last night gave us something to think about, that's for sure. Glad you remembered to hide that book under the back of your shirt. Mr. Demming probably wouldn't have let us take it."

"I know. He sure is strange. Real business like."

"I know. Glad my dad isn't like that," Willie said.

"Me, too."

"So first thing I think we should do is try to find that last known relative, what's his name? A…a..Polchet. There was nothing that gave a died date so he must still be alive. And now that we know it was called Sudbury House, we should be able to find more information on that in the historical archives at the library and the county offices in Old Brunswicktown."

"Want some coffee?" Kurt asked

"Sure." Willie stuffed more waffle in his mouth and watched Kurt fill the coffee mugs and fetch the sugar. "Thanks. And besides," he continued, "that was pretty rude of them to kick us out before we even had anything to eat. I sure am glad I'm not rich because I would never want to be that rude."

"No kidding!"

"As far as when we can get to Old Brunswicktown, we'll work that out with Madison. She mentioned Wednesday. Sounds like a good a day as any. Oh, hi Mom, hi Dad," Willie called when his parents came home.

"Hi Mrs. M, Mr. M," Kurt said.

"Hello boys. How was last night? They didn't feed you there?" Barbara McLeish entered the kitchen while her husband saw to putting away their coats and scarfs. She scooped up the dishes from the table.

"It went okay. Did my dad tell you what happened?" Kurt asked. He followed his plate to the sink and scooped up the last of his waffle before Mrs. McLeish set the dish in the sink.

"Yes he did. I think it was good of both of you boys to stay if that girl was that frightened," Barbara added. She poured herself a mug of coffee.

"Yeah, she was pretty scared, but the nurse gave her mom a sedative and she slept through the night. We ended up talking with Madison and her friend Zola until nearly four this morning about stuff," Willie added. "Did you know who moved in that old manor, Mom? Their last name is Demming, I guess her mom is Rozlin... Rozlin Demming."

Barbara McLeish's cold pink cheeks turned white and the coffee mug dropped from her hand, hitting the floor with a crash, breaking the mug and sending shards of glass and hot coffee everywhere.

"Mom! Look out!" Willie jumped out of the way. "Are you all right?" he stared at her shocked face.

"What is it, Lovie?" Her husband entered the kitchen when he heard the crash. He eased her away from the mess on the floor.

"I..I... goodness I don't know what happened! I guess my fingers were still cold from outside." She gave a weak laugh.

"We'll get this. You go warm up and we'll bring you some fresh coffee, all right?" Kurt said. She nodded, as though in a daze, and Ian led her out of the kitchen.

"Thank you boys...I guess I will. I guess I must be worn out what with this Christmas bazaar at the church and all the decorating and that surprise baby shower I am planning for you mom next week. I...I think I will just lie down for a moment."

Willie watched his mom and dad disappear up the stairs before turning to Kurt. He said, "What was that all about?"

"I don't know but it looked like she sure was scared about something. Your dad will make sure she's okay. Let's get this cleaned up, then we'll head to my house and see how my mom is doing, all right?"

"Sure, oh hey Dad! Mom all right?"

"Yes, I don't know what came over her. But she's resting."

"Here is a fresh cup for Mom, and one for you." Willie handed his dad the steaming mugs while Kurt finished moping the floor.

"Thanks, boys, and make sure your homework is done and there's a dusting on those steps out back to clean, Willie."

"No problem, Dad. We'll take care of all that."

It was quiet when Kurt and Willie entered the Brandon home and they quickly removed their jackets and boots and started for the kitchen. There was Robert Brandon bent over the counter top staring at a small 3 x 5 piece of paper so absorbed he didn't hear the boys come in.

"What you got there, Dad?" Kurt stuck his head in the space between the paper and his dad's head.

"Kurt!" his dad jumped back. "You startled me! Should never sneak up on a cop that way, son."

"We didn't mean to, Mr. B." Willie finally managed after he and Kurt finished laughing.

"So where's Mom?"

"Upstairs resting. It seems the closer that baby's due date gets the more tired she gets. I told her I would make supper tonight."

"Ohhhhhhhhhhhh! So that's what's on the card. Let's see," Kurt spun the card around. "Meatloaf! I love meatloaf, but since when do you need a recipe?"

"All right that's enough. I'm not the cook your mother is so I need all the help I can get. So tell me what happened with your stay at Pine Manor."

"It's Towering Pines Manor, Mr. B," Willie corrected and grabbed an apple. "That's what we came to talk to you about."

"Really?"

"Yes, we have several questions for you about this new case we're working on and…"

"Case? Just several months ago it was mischief and adventure now it's actual cases huh?" Brandon smiled.

"Well, we're older and wiser now and we figured we can start calling them cases, Dad. So, the first question is, did Deputy Calhoun find any tracks back there?"

"No he didn't, but then he was only able to get part way because of the snowbanks. But he did say there was nothing as far as he could see in the beam of his flashlight."

"Wish he would have gone around because I did see someone, Dad."

"Was this someone going away from the house or towards the house?" Brandon asked. He poured himself a cup of coffee and sat at the table with the boys, his curiosity piqued.

"Towards. He was hunched over like he was in a hurry, and don't go telling me it was bigfoot or something because Willie already tried that."

"Okay, towards the house. How long before you heard Mrs. Demming scream?"

"I'd say about three maybe four minutes wouldn't you Kurt?" Willie said. "Richard was driving and he isn't the fastest Mario Andretti on the block if you get my drift. He was going slow because of the ice on the road and those s curves are pretty sssy so he was going pretty slow."

"Sure, I would say about three to four minutes. That would give the guy plenty of time to get to the house, get inside, sneak up to Mrs. Demming's room and scare the heck out of her, right?" Kurt asked.

"I suppose so. But that would raise the question, where did he gain entrance from?" Brandon asked.

"That's why Deputy Calhoun should have gone all the way around," Kurt chastised. "But don't worry, Dad, we can do that. We're not afraid of trudging through deep snow. We do it all the time, right Will?"

"Right. Then the next question is, was Mrs. Demming able at all to identify the intruder?" Willie asked.

"No. You heard what I heard. That she woke up and he was standing near the door to the sitting room. He was all dressed in black, black hat and black cover over his face. Then he disappeared."

"So, she wasn't even able to determine whether it was a man or a woman?" Kurt cried.

"No....actually not. But it still leaves the question, where did he disappear to."

"We checked it twice, Dad. Knocked on all the walls, looked under every chair and sofa and even looked under all those covers they have over the tables. Nothing, nada, zilch but that door behind that tapestry."

"So if he used that door, how did he get past all of you on the stairs?" Kurt's dad asked.

"Don't know." Willie shrugged and tossed his core in the trash. "But it's like I said yesterday, he could have waited until we were all past and in Mrs. Demming's room before he even escaped."

"That's true and most likely the case. But that begs the question, where did he go from there? Any more questions?" Brandon asked.

"We're working on all that, Dad." Kurt looked at Willie who gave him that encouraging nod.

"And, we were wondering if you checked up on anyone, you know like the nurse or the driver? Madison told us that Richard has been her driver for over ten years and came from some foreign country. That old grey-haired woman, Agnes has been with her mom since she was born and she wouldn't hurt a fly. If anyone tried to hurt Mrs. Demming, Agnes would probably go ballistic on them," Kurt said.

"Yes, Madison also said that Nurse Winthrop was only hired recently when they came here. Madison says she has complete control over what Mrs. Demming takes for drugs and what she does and who can and can't see her, and Madison says…"

"Goodness!" Brandon exclaimed. "Madison sure says a lot!"

"*OH*! You have no idea!" Kurt cried out with a laugh.

"All right then, I am guessing you suspect the nurse? Why?"

"Because she just looks suspicious and she acts suspicious. I mean, what nurse in this day and age is as rude as all that? It's like she owns Mrs. Demming. Even Madison has to ask permission!" Willie cried. "And don't forget, she wasn't the first one in Mrs. Demming's room!"

"Look, Dad, is there any way you can check up on her? And we were also wondering if you could find out who owns the house. We found a paper that says the last surviving relative there was a guy named Tobias Polchet but there was nothing to say where he was or what he did for a living."

"As much as I would love to help you boys now that you have a real case and all, but I can't use the resources of the police department to search out information for you, you know that. But that Polchet name sounds familiar. I think I remember Cliff talking about him once. Cliff's wife works at the senior home in Old Brunswicktown. I'm pretty sure they were talking about a really unsociable guy that just celebrated his 90 something birthday. That might be him."

"That's a start, Mr. B, thanks."

"Good, now if you boys will get out of my kitchen, I have supper to prepare."

"It's not even noon, Dad!"

"It's going to take me that long to figure this out. Now out! Both of you. Here, bring this juice and crackers up to your mother and get out of my hair!"

Kurt laughed. "I sure am glad he doesn't cook all the time. We'd probably never eat!"

"I've been thinking. Let's go upstairs and check on your mom and then go see Mrs. Hendicott. I'll bet she knows about this Polchet guy. And let's bring the book."

"Great idea. Hi Mom! How you feeling?"

"Hi Mrs. B. We just wanted to drop this off then we're going to visit Mrs. Hendicott. Mr. B says you need your rest."

"Thanks boys but before you leave, bring me that book over there would you, Willie. Tell your father where you're going." She settled back with the book.

The Hidden Secret of Towering Pines Manor

Chapter Ten

"So it sure looks like your mom is getting pretty big!" Willie said on their way to Mrs. Hendicott's.

"I know. Sometimes she has trouble getting out of the chair and my dad has to help her. I sure hope that kid isn't going to weigh a ton!"

"So, do you know if it's a boy or a girl?" Willie tossed a snowball into the air.

"No. My mom and dad said they didn't want to know what the ultra-sound showed because they want to wait for nature to tell us what the baby is. All they care about at this point is that the baby is doing okay."

"And is it? Okay I mean?"

"Yes, so far so good, according to my mom."

"Any names yet?"

"They've been tossing around some names like Maria and Rose and Heather."

"Sounds like they are hoping for a girl."

"I think so. Mom is always telling me she couldn't stay sane if there was another one like me."

"She's probably right."

"I told them I think Catherine Jane would be good. Then we could call her CJ and she'd be just like a little brother anyway."

Willie laughed. "What'd they say to that?"

"My mom threw her book at me." They plowed through the snow and turned onto Mrs. Hendicott's walkway. They quickly grabbed the shovels that were leaning against the inside of the door and scraped the sidewalk clean from the dusting that had accumulated over night.

"Hey, Mrs. Hendicott!" Willie shouted in through the door. The boys stomped the snow from their boots and removed their jackets. Mrs. Hendicott emerged from the kitchen with seven cats trailing behind her. Already the smell of roast chicken was in the air.

"I see your fan club is checking on supper with you, huh?" Kurt grinned.

"Oh my goodness yes. These little stinkers are out of control!" Mrs. Hendicott laughed. "Course they know what goodies are for supper tonight. Chicken is their favorite. Oh, what have you there, Kurt?" She noticed the book beneath his arm.

"Come on in and sit down. Have we got a story to tell you!" he cried.

"I'll get the hot chocolate," Willie shouted from the kitchen.

"You boys certainly know how to spoil an old woman," Mrs. Hendicott smiled. She sat in her favorite chair, Alexander the Great sprawled on the rug before the blazing fire. Tabitha, the fluffy white Birman settled next to Kurt along with Calista, another fluffy white Persian. The green-eyed Siamese Tiffany, curled around Mrs. Hendicott's feet and the smoky brown mixed breed Tom, vied for the cushioned arms of the sofa with three other purring mixes. Willie entered with a tray of steaming chocolate and cookies.

"Found these on the counter! They look so good. Did Kurt tell you?"

"No, we were waiting for you," Mrs. Hendicott accepted a mug of chocolate and small plate of cookies. "What is so exciting about this book?"

"Look here!" Kurt held the book before her so she could see. He flipped the pages and continued, "This is a book of the genealogy of the people who lived up at Towering Pines Manor, only it wasn't Towering Pines Manor when it was built. It was called Sudbury House and there have been generations of people living there. Look at all the pictures! And look at this one all the way in the back! The guy must have hated his wife because he tore up her picture!"

"Slow down, Kurt, my eyes aren't as good as they used to be. Turn those pages slower and let me read." Mrs. Hendicott moved from page to page, from face to face, from description to description until Kurt's arms were ready to fall off. Finally, she leaned back and sighed. "Yes, I do remember my grandfather speaking of that house. I remember he told us of all the deaths there, but back then, there were illnesses and diseases that weren't curable at the time. Death was an everyday occurrence and we thought nothing of it. But I remember this one time when I was a little girl, a group of us, oh goodness we were only in primer school then, but we got together and we went up to that house. It was so different then, what with all those trees surrounding it, that huge black fence. We managed to get in and we actually got into the house with nobody noticing. It was on a dare, and no one ever backed down from a dare." Kurt and Willie grinned at each other. They knew exactly what she meant.

"We were running around and laughing and, oh yes, there was a solarium I believe, and there were so many plants and the water fountain was so beautiful. No! Wait just a moment. That's not right either. Yes…yes…that's it. The solarium wasn't there. They were just building it. That's how we managed to get in because there were workers and supply trucks coming and going. But they had all the construction materials there and the fountain had been connected just to make sure it was going to work. I remember, all of us girls took our shoes off and we were playing in the fountain and suddenly a door opened from the side of the house and this giant of a man all dressed in black came up. When he saw us he started shouting and raising his fist and he chased us out. We were so frightened we forgot to pick up our shoes. One of the girls got into a lot of trouble for that. My grandfather just laughed and said he was proud of my bravery because he said the house was haunted and anyone who goes inside never comes out alive."

"Wait a minute, you said this man dressed in black came up through the door. Was it the front door?" Kurt asked.

"No, there was another door not too far from the front door. He came up from there."

"You mean down from the stairs, don't you?" Willie asked.

"No dear. He came up some stairs through the door. I remember because when he pulled the door open, all we could see at first was his head and shoulders and then the rest of him came up. It was definitely up the stairs."

"Where was this door? I'm asking because when we were in there yesterday all we found was the one door that led to a set of stairs going up at the far end of the room," Willie added.

"This door, if I recall correctly, was more towards that part of the wall that jutted inward and joined with the wall of the foyer."

"But there isn't a door there now, because we looked," Kurt said.

"I'm telling you there was a door there. There's a cellar on that house and everyone was afraid to go there. Not even workmen would go down there. That's why when it was renovated, one of the rooms was changed over into the utility room where the new heating system and all the electrical and plumbing was installed."

"Well, it could have been removed when they added the solarium, too," Willie said.

"We didn't even see the utility room." Kurt set the book down and rubbed his arms.

"It's in the hall near the library. I guess they wanted it centrally located in the house."

"How do you know that, Mrs. Hendicott, about the room and the basement and all that?" Kurt asked.

"I remember Horace speaking of it. He worked as a bank clerk you see and when anything happened in Fisherman's Haven, everyone knew about it. It was no secret."

"So," Kurt cast Willie a meaningful glance, "there's another door in that room and there's a cellar. Very interesting!"

"Do you know anything about that last surviving relative, that Tobias Polchet guy?" Willie asked.

"Oh yes, now that you mention it. That was his name. I guess I was mixed up with someone else. But yes, James Polchet... James Polchet... that was the father's name. He wasn't an original Sudbury and he wasn't from around these parts if I recall. Came from out west, Chicago I think. Drove out here in one of those new contraptions called an automobile, a Ford automobile, black and shiny as a raven it was, so Grandfather told us. He courted the daughter of that manor house and won her over with his city ways and fancy talk, and it wasn't long before they were married. His name was Polchet...James Polchet. Yes...yes... He married the daughter and they had a son, Tobias."

"So this Tobias Polchet, did he ever get married?" Willie asked.

"No...no I don't think he ever did. He lived in that house with his father until the old man died, and then he changed the name to Towering Pines Manor. Goodness! Just talking about this has brought back so many memories! I'd forgotten most of this until just now."

"So what happened to this James Polchet's wife, the original daughter of the manor?" Kurt asked.

"Oh, they say she ran away and after that it was pretty hush hush about anything coming from that house."

"So you don't know what happened to her or to the son, Tobias?" Kurt asked.

"No, but as I said, Tobias lived there for a while and then abandoned the place. I think he still owns it but it's been near fifty or more years since he left. They say he was a little crazy from living there with his father for so long."

"Do you think that could be the Polchet that is in that nursing home in Old Brunswicktown?"Willie asked. "You know, the one Kurt's dad mentioned."

"Could be... you boys sure have found out a lot about that manor house. So is it haunted like they say?" Mrs. Hendicott asked with a gleam in her eye.

"We don't know for sure. But there are a lot of strange noises all over the place," Willie said with a shiver. "Would you like me to heat up more hot chocolate?"

"No thank you, dear. I've had plenty. It'll ruin my supper. But I am glad you both stopped to visit."

"Thanks, Mrs. Hendicott. You've been a big help. Now we have a good place to start again." Kurt gathered up the plates and mugs and carried the tray to the kitchen.

"Leave the dishes, boys. I will get them later," called Mrs. Hendicott.

"Okay, thanks. We'll have to get going. We'll let you know how things turn out."

"Bye!" Mrs. Hendicott smiled and glanced to the urn with the black kitty paws on the mantle.

Chapter Eleven

"I am so glad we don't have school this afternoon," Willie laughed.

"Me, too, I love it when they have in-service teaching for the teachers." The boys bounded down the stairs of the school two at a time.

"Hey you guys! Wait up!" Madison shouted from the door. She hurried to catch up. "So what do you say we take the afternoon and go to Old Brunswicktown and check the deeds office."

"I don't think we need to check the deeds office, but we could just to be sure that Tobias Polchet still owns the place," Kurt said. "We found out more information from my dad and Mrs. Hendicott."

"Like what?" Madison fell into step with them until they reached the corner. There was Richard waiting beside the Chrysler 310.

"So you don't really walk all the way to school, huh?" Willie grinned.

"Of course not!" Madison laughed. "Hold up, we have to wait for Zola."

"Oh, is she coming, too?" Willie asked with a rolled eye to Kurt.

"Of course. We are in this together. Oh look, there she is. Zola!" Madison shouted and waived her arm. Zola hurried over.

"So what are we doing today? Back to the manor?" Zola asked.

"No, we're going to Old Brunswicktown today instead of Wednesday to check on that deed and make a stop at the nursing home there." Willie toned down to a whisper when they neared the car.

"Why are we whispering?" Zola asked glancing about.

"We don't want anyone to know, not even Richard."

"Why? We can trust him," Madison said defensively.

"No, we can't," Willie whispered. "While we are investigating we trust no one, everyone is a suspect."

"Like you guys are P.I.'s or something," Madison scoffed.

"Look!" Kurt pulled her around and everyone came to a halt. "Do you want our help or not? If not, see ya. If yes, then we do it our way, got it?"

"Okay, I didn't mean to....."

"Please let's not argue!" Zola pleaded.

"Look, let's just get going. First we are going to head home and let our folks know where we are going. Second we are all going to have some lunch cause it might be a long day," Willie said. "Come on, Kurt."

"Wait a minute," Madison called hoping to redeem herself. "Richard can give us all a ride home and we'll come back around say about 1:30 to pick everyone up again? Is that going to be enough time?"

"Sure. That's okay." They all climbed in the back seat and sat silent. Richard got behind the wheel, cast a wary look in the rear view mirror and shook his head.

"Hey Mom!" Willie shouted when he and Kurt stomped in through the kitchen. "We only had a half day of school today because of teacher training. We already cleared it with Mrs. B so is it all right if we go to Old Brunswicktown with a couple of friends?"

"Oh, hello boys. I don't see why not. Oh!" Barbara McLeish turned towards the knock on the door. "I'll get the door, you boys get your own lunch."

When she was out of hearing distance, Willie whispered, "That was easy! Grab the PBJ and I'll get the bread and milk. So where do you think we should go first? Deeds office or nursing home?"

"I think the nursing home first seeing as we already know Tobias Polchet still owns the place. If that old man is there, he might be able to answer a lot of questions. If not, it will only have wasted a few minutes of our time." Kurt brought the bread and jars to the table and jumped when a shout came from the front hall. "Hey, was that your mom?"

"Yeah! Something must have scared her. Let's check."

The boys started toward the hall but stopped when they saw Mrs. McLeish standing at the door. There was a tall man barring the way, his arms spread across the opening. The boys ducked and craned their heads to listen.

"Wha...what are you doing here?" Barbara McLeish's voice was strained and shaky. "How did you find us?"

"So this is where you've gotten off to. I knew all along you'd never amount to anything since you got caught up with that Irishman. Look at you!" He threw his hands in the air and Barbara McLeish flinched backwards. "A pathetic waste of life. What are you supposed to be? A housewife! What!" he shouted in her face.

Barbara backed up several steps. She threw her hands to her mouth to muffle her startled cry. It had been so long since she'd seen him, so long since the nightmares of his tyrannical manipulations had disturbed her. Now it was all coming back and she felt once more like that bullied, dominated little frightened girl she'd become once her mom had died.

"You are disgusting. If you'd only done what I told you to do. But no....no you were just as loose and stupid as your mother. She was nothing! And you've followed in her footsteps!" growled the man at the door. "I should have known you'd be nothing but a common whore!"

"Get out!" Barbara finally screamed. "Get out and never come back! We ran away once and we don't want you in our lives! Get out!" She somehow found the courage to push the man backwards and slam the door. She was shaking and looked frantically about her, looking for a place to run, a place to hide. But this was her house, her life. She sat on the stairs and burst into sobs.

"Mom!" Willie ran to her. "Mom what was that all about? Who was that man?"

"Oh, William!" She sobbed and ran up the stairs, the door to her bedroom slamming shut.

"Willie?" Kurt called out, but he was too late. Willie had already thrown the door open with such force it hit the bottom stair and bounced back almost taking off the hand Kurt had put out to catch it. Willie was livid. His face was burning with anger and his hands were already balling into fists as he stomped towards the retreating figure.

"Hey you!" Willie shouted. "Hey you!" He gripped the man by the shoulder and spun him around. The man stood at least a foot taller than Willie, a tall lanky man with greying hair and a long patrician nose that stank of money. He stared with derision at the fuming boy in front of him.

"Oh I understand," the man said with a sneer. "She sends out a boy to handle her mess! I see the red hair and cocky look about you. You must be the illegitimate one! You look just like your father!"

Willie's lips pursed in anger and his fingers tightened into the hardest fist he could ever have deemed possible. He pulled his arm back with sudden swiftness, the fingers coiled to tight white knots. He did not realize that he had punched the man in the face until he looked down and saw him lying flat on his back on the wet sidewalk, blood dripping from his nose and mouth.

In an instant, Willie dropped to his knees and grabbed the man by the tie yanking his face inches from his own. He could smell the starched whiteness of the man's shirt. He could smell the expensive aftershave. He could smell the subtle hint of tobacco, and it all made him sick. "I don't care who you are. I don't care what you do. Nobody comes here and talks to my mom that way. Nobody ever comes here and makes her cry. You get the hell out of here and don't ever come back!" Willie thrust him back, stood up and spit on the ground. "Get out of here!" Then he turned and stalked back into the house.

The driver of the car scrambled out when he saw the man emerge from the house. He had opened the back door, but was now staring open-mouthed at the sheer audacity of the tall, thin red-headed boy who had punched the man in the face and now stalked away, fists tightening over and over at his side. The driver smiled before he went to help the man from the sidewalk.

Kurt stood in the opened doorway, his mouth hanging open.

"Catching flies!" Willie demanded. He pushed Kurt out of the way and slammed the door shut. He leaned back against the door and closed his eyes. He willed himself to breathe easy, to calm himself and it was several minutes before he felt the anger begin to soothe away. He opened his eyes and saw Kurt leaning against the stair rail, looking in every direction but his. "Look, Kurt, I am sorry. That rotten guy out there really made me mad. Making my mom cry like that."

"I thought you were pretty lenient."

"Man! I wanted to hurt that guy!"

"I could tell!"

"My poor mom."

"Do you think she's okay?"

"I'm going to check. It must be something really bad because the only time she calls me William is when she is really upset."

"Maybe we should leave her alone," Kurt suggested.

"No!" Willie shouted, his anger rising once more. "I'm tired of not knowing about the past. I'm tired of being treated like some little kid who won't understand. Everything about their past is so secretive and after her cup dropping incident when I mentioned Rozlin Demming and now this? No, I really have to know what is going on."

"All right. You want me to come with you or not?"

"Come. I'm going to tell you everything anyway."

Kurt shrugged and followed Willie up the stairs. He waited at the landing when Willie stopped at his mom's door and wretchedly listened to the sobs within. Willie tapped on the door and called in, "Mom? Can we come in?"

Barbara McLeish had flown up the stairs through blinding tears. She had slammed the door behind her, too frightened and ashamed to face anyone. She reached for the tissue box and ignored the knocking on the door. But Willie was insistent, and soon she could not ignore the concern in his voice. She wiped her face and pulled herself up to lean against the back of the bed. "Oh, come in." Willie inched into the room and she continued, "And , don't look so glum, I'm all right."

"Who was that man anyway, Mom?"

"It…it ….it was your grandfather. That's my father."

"Your dad? My grandfather? Oh geez, I just punched him in the face, Mom!" Willie exclaimed.

"Nothing less than what he deserved, if you ask me," Kurt said. He shut his mouth when he saw the look Willie's mom gave him.

"So what is going on, Mom. First that thing with the cup when I mentioned Rozlin Demming and now this guy shows up and makes you cry. What's in your past that I don't know about. What's in your past that I *should* know about."

"It's such a long story, Willie." Barbara pulled the box of tissues near.

"Well, we have roughly a half hour, plenty of time, right?" Willie grinned at her.

"Oh stop that silly grinning," Barbara finally smiled a little. "I guess you have a right to know the truth. I think it's about time you know what happened. Your father and I were hoping to never have to tell you, and if the time ever came, we wanted to tell you together."

"Yeah, well Dad won't be home for another six hours and by that time you'll find some excuse not to tell me so out with it. I'm not a kid anymore, Mom. Geez, I'm going to be sixteen soon. Don't you think I deserve to know?"

Barbara McLeish searched her son's face.

"Please, Mom!" Willie reached for her hand and gave it a squeeze. She sighed and shrugged.

"You're right. You're absolutely right. It all was so long ago, when I was a little girl. My father was rich, very rich, and he married into more money when he married my mother. She was a lawyer and he managed stocks on Wall Street. They were friends with Barry Kruger and his wife Jackie and of course, their daughter Rozlin and I grew up to be best friends. But then when my mother died, I was eleven at the time, my dad became so strict. He began to dictate who I could go out with, where I could go, what I was supposed to do with my life. The only time I felt like a normal girl was the time I spent with Rozlin. When I was with her, we would dance and laugh and sing to stupid songs on the radio. We even slipped out a few times and went to forbidden nightclubs! By the time we were ready for college, Rozlin was already dating a law student named Collin Demming and I was dating the son of one of my father's partners, Todd something or other. Course that was all right because he was my dad's partner's son. The money thing, you know?

"It happened this one night that we were coming home from a club when the tire blew out on our car and we crashed into the side of a building. Todd was so drunk that he just passed out in the front seat. He had driven recklessly into a poor neighborhood , and I was so frightened. Then out of nowhere this tall, red- headed man pulls over in his beat up

Chevy and asked if I needed help. I was so frightened! I didn't know him! He had this heavy Irish accent and I could barely understand him. But when I looked at him offering me help and then over to Todd slumped over the wheel, I accepted his help. I called for a tow truck to pick Todd and his car up, and I let that Irish man take me home. Needless to say, I met him over and over and soon we began to date.

"I would never tell my father because Ian was poor. He was a foreigner with no money, a low paying job and going to school at night. Someone my father would never stand for. But we knew we were in love and Rozlin would say I was with her when I was really with Ian. Then I discovered that I was....." she glanced to Willie's face then down to the hands folded in her lap. "I discovered that I was pregnant. When I told Ian, I was afraid he would push me away or worse yet suggest an abortion, but he was so happy and excited! He wanted to get married right away. So we hatched a plan that I was going to go to Rozlin's and Ian was going to come and get me there, just like always. But when we got there, there were four men that grabbed Ian and they beat him very badly! My father grabbed hold of me and pushed me into the car and locked me in my room when we got home until he found out that I was pregnant. Then he threw me out!"

"Oh Mom!" Willie grabbed hold of her hand and squeezed.

"I...I didn't know where to go or where to turn. I tried to find Ian but he had been beaten so badly I didn't know he was in the hospital. I went to Rozlin's and it was then that she told me how sorry she was for what happened. She said she didn't know what my father was going to do! She said that he promised to get her fiancé, Collin, a partnership in a big law firm if she told him what I was up to, so she had been spying on me and telling my father everything!"

"Oh man, no wonder you dropped your cup when we mentioned her name," Kurt said.

"Yes. She was my best friend and she had betrayed me. Not only me, but Ian as well and our baby.....you." She smiled at Willie.

"So then what happened?" Willie squeezed her hand and smiled.

"Roz told me Ian was in the hospital and I went there. He didn't have any money so they were discharging him when I got there. He brought me to his apartment and I stayed there until he finished school. He only had two weeks to graduation and I didn't want to be the reason why he failed to graduate. Once he was finished, we were married at the court house and moved to the other side of New York, then finally here. How were we to know he would find us here!" she cried.

"Oh man, Mom. That's probably our fault," Willie stared at her.

"What do you mean? How could that possibly be your fault?"

"We are helping Madison Demming with something and we were at her house the other day when her father came home. I thought he looked at me kind of queer like and now I know the reason. He probably recognized the name and when he looked at me, recognized that I look like dad. He probably called your dad and told him where we were."

"Oh dear, you may be right."

"I just punched him square in the face, Mom! Do you think he's going to make trouble for dad? I mean like beat him up again or maybe get him fired?" Willie groaned.

"Oh, I don't think so, honey. So much time has passed. I think the only reason he came here was to humiliate me and to let me know that he knew where we were and show that he still has control."

"Control over what?"

"Over me, over Ian, over everything. My father is the sort of man who always has to be in control. And that's why he disowned me. He finally realized he couldn't control me any longer. This was an attempt to humiliate me once more, to see if I would beg for forgiveness...."

"Beg for forgiveness!" Willie jumped from the bed and cried out angrily. "From him? Don't you ever dare, Mom and don't you ever expect me to forgive him either!"

"Oh, William, we must find it in our hearts to forgive yes, even him," Barbara McLeish said noting the anger in Willie's eyes.

"Are *you* going to? Did you already? Doesn't what he did today show you he doesn't deserve forgiveness, Mom?"

"Everyone always deserves forgiveness, Will, it's what Jesus would want from all of us."

"Maybe. Maybe a hundred years from now, you can ask me that again. But not now, not right now, Mom, not after what he's done to you and Dad. Anyway, I told him to get the heck out of here and never come back. I can see why you never told me about him. What a jerk!"

"But he is still your grandfather and he is so wealthy he could do a lot for you, you know."

"I don't want his money, Mom. I don't want any part of him if he's that way. He can just stay in New York and leave us alone. We're better off without him. We've managed so far, haven't we?"

"So....you...you aren't holding judgment over our mistakes?"

"Mistakes? What mistakes. Oh! Did you think that being pregnant first then getting married was going to upset me? Come on, Mom! This is the twenty-first century. I don't care one bit. All I care is that you're my mom and Dad is my dad. Can't ask for better than that!" he grinned.

"Oh, William, come here!" Barbara pulled him towards her and gripped him in a huge bear hug.

"MMMMom!" Willie laughed and pulled away. "We still have to go have something to eat. Madison is picking us up any minute to go to Old Brunswicktown. Need us to pick up anything for you? Are you going to be all right? Should I call someone to come over?"

"No, I'm fine. I'm just fine. You two go ahead. I'm going to wash my face and think of something special for supper. You know, to celebrate."

"Great, see you later, Mom!"

"See you, Mrs. M," Kurt yelled and followed Willie down the stairs.

"Whew! Can you believe that? Rozlin Demming was my mom's best friend?"

"And worse, a traitor?" Kurt added. "Doggone it! There's Richard honking that horn already. Grab the PBJs and let's get going."

The boys piled in the car and scrunched in between Zola and Madison and Richard drove off without a word.

"What's going on?" Madison asked. "You guys look angry about something."

"Oh, nothing, just a little family matter."

"And an hour wasn't enough to eat in?" she asked eyeing their crumbs as they ate.

"Nope, just too much going on. We'll be done by the time we get there. Don't worry," Willie said through a mouthful of sandwich.

It was half an hour before they turned into the parking lot of the only nursing home in Old Brunswicktown, The Happy Golden Years, of which the name alone was a misnomer for nobody there appeared to be happy at being old. The building was a renovated brown stone that looked just as ancient and crumbly as it did before the renovation. The only obvious telltale signs were wheelchair ramps and gleaming yellow railings.

It was a warm afternoon and the sun glistened across the snow with a blinding glare. The four of them shielded their eyes and ducked quickly beneath the canopy that covered the entrance. They hesitated, reluctant to enter. Peering through a large window into a very small room, they saw residents crowded everywhere.

"Can I help you?" They jumped when a nurse approached.

"Yes, maybe you can. We were told that a Mr. Tobias Polchet is here?" Madison spoke up.

"There." The nurse pointed through the window to a lone man in the corner.

"Thanks," they all muttered.

"You won't get much out of him, though," the nurse said.

"Why's that?" Willie asked.

"He's as loony as the day is long." She turned smartly and walked away.

They threaded through the maze of wheelchairs and tables of card playing seniors to the corner table where Tobias Polchet sat.

He was alone. His shriveled and gnarled hands twined before him on the table. His hair was full and grey, and stood straight up as though he'd run his hands through it over and over. His eyes were tiny ovals in shrunken sockets hidden deep within the folds of the high cheek bones and the thin lips moved as if in prayer. He leaned forward, peering through the window, searching the grounds as though he expected someone to be there.

"Ah, are you Mr. Polchet? Mr. Tobias Polchet?" Kurt asked tentatively.

"What of it!" The man jerked his head up and snarled at them. They all jumped back.

"We...we were wondering if we could visit with you, that's all," Zola said.

"I see. You come for my money, they all come for my money!" Tobias Polchet growled.

"We don't want your money sir, we just wanted to talk to you about your family, about your house in Fisherman's Haven," Willie said.

"House? That's no house! It's a curse is what it is! Sit down! Don't be standing around looking like fools! What are you staring at?" He shouted around him but no one was really paying him any attention.

"Sorry," Kurt muttered and they all pulled out a chair and sat as far on the opposite side of the table as they could scrunch their chairs together.

"I don't like it here. They tell me what to do and want my money," Polchet said. He leaned forward and peered to the left, then the right, then whispered "but on Sunday, we have chocolate cake for dessert!" Then he laughed. He caught himself and looked guiltily around as though he had done something wrong. Then he turned to stare once more out the window.

"Okay, um, we wanted to know if you still own Towering Pines Manor," Willie said.

"Towering Pines? Of course I own Towering Pines, you little upstart! Who do you think would own Towering Pines! It's been in my family for generations! It was built by my family. Damn fool boy! Of course I own Towering Pines Manor!"

"So how come you don't live there?" Willie asked.

Tobias Polchet sat bolt upright in the wheelchair startling everyone. For just an instant, terror gripped him, then his eyes narrowed slightly, he leaned forward conspiratorially and in a hoarse whisper he said, "Because that damn infernal place is haunted! They were after me, all of them, I had to get away!"

"Who? Who was after you?" Kurt asked.

"Them! Them ghosts everywhere!"

"There are ghosts there?" Madison asked.

"What? What is that lass?...did I tell you," Polchet's voice suddenly softened, "that on Sunday we have chocolate cake for dessert?" And he laughed.

"Oh brother!" Willie clapped his hand to his forehead.

"Mr. Polchet," Zola spoke softly, "would you mind telling us about your parents? About the time when you were a little boy and lived at Towering Pines Manor?"

"Of course, little lass, of course. I was born there and grew up there. Mind now it was not called Towering Pines Manor. Oh no. Sudbury House. That's what it was called. Sudbury House," he repeated with disdain.

"I hated that place. I wasn't happy there. Not by a long shot. My father was a cruel and harsh man living strictly by the laws of the land and the good book. He was cruel in his punishments, he was."

"What about your mother?" Madison finally ventured a question.

"I remember my father, yes I do. He was a tall man. Towered over me, he did. A mean spiteful man, always ready with the switch and that switch didn't rest for too long. He found reasons to use that switch he did!"

Madison gulped and asked again. "And what about your mother? Did he beat her? Did he beat her like he beat you?"

"What is that you brash young whip! My mother! Bah! Don't speak of that whore to me!" he spat at her. "That....that whore! Married to my father and whoring around with someone else. My father knew, he told me that was why she left. Deserted us! Ran off with that lover of hers, he said!"

"She ran away?" Madison asked.

"Where did they go? What happened to them?" Willie asked.

Tobias Polchet's mouth opened as if to speak, his face paled and twisted as though he were pleading for help. He was a man lost in time and he turned towards the window remembering the switch, remembering the house, his mind struggling to remember his mother. Dancing shadows, soft footsteps, the humming of a lullaby and the soft whimpering of a baby clouded his memory. He squeezed his eyes and tried to shake off the visions, but they persisted. Suddenly the vision of a beautiful woman with long dark hair arose. She swayed as if in a dream, a small child sleeping at her shoulder. She was shaking her head, telling him no, telling him it was all wrong, telling him......he jerked his eyes wide open and stared into the faces of the four in front of him and smiled. "Did I tell you on Sunday we have chocolate cake for dessert?"

"Yes, you did. You must like chocolate cake," Zola said. "Did your mother make you chocolate cake?"

"That whore!" he shouted again. "Don't know and don't much care. She was a whore and once she was gone my father forbade me to speak of her or mention her ever again!"

"Wow! So she never came back?" Kurt asked.

Tobias Polchet slammed his fist on the table with a strength that seemed unlikely he could possess. Everyone jumped. "What did I just tell you boy! Never mention that whore!"

"Geez, sorry!" Kurt nearly flipped backwards in his chair.

"Did I tell you that on Sunday we have chocolate cake? Best dessert of the week. All those other days we have trash, like jello or pudding. Bah! But I remember...yes, yes I remember, it was several years later, I was ten or twelve and my father was having an exceptionally out of sorts day. I found a comb that belonged to...to *her*, and when I approached my father with it he flew into such a rage! Locked me in the cellar for two days. *Two days*! In the darkness. With them! I knew then I would never mention *her* again. It was dark there and they were there! All of them, whispering, laughing, crying in my head. The cellar is haunted you know. I never questioned my father again. No, not even when he was old and crippled."

"Is that why you don't live there?" Willie asked.

"I lived there long after my father died. For many years I listened to them, to the whisperings and the sound of footsteps and children crying. I even changed the name to Towering Pines Manor, but it made no never mind. I felt I owed it to the family name to stay, to make something of it. But they wanted me out of there. They made me go. They made me leave. I want no part of that place!"

"But you still own it and people rent it," Madison said.

"Yes they do, but no one stays. Those ghosts scare them off. I'd just as soon sell it, get rid of it, burn it down, but they won't let me. Not until the truth is discovered."

"Truth! What truth?" Willie asked leaning forward.

"Who? Who won't let you? Who won't let you do what?" Madison asked.

"The truth of all of it. My father, them! It's them ghosts! They come here, they do. Not a moment's rest. It's them won't let me sell!"

"So if someone rents it, then you must have a caretaker or somebody that rents it out for you, right?" Kurt asked.

"Nah! My lawyer sees to all that legal rigamarole."

"Then who is your lawyer, if we might ask?" Kurt asked.

"Some high falutin' character from Boston. Comes here to see me once maybe twice a year, pays my expenses and takes his exorbitant fees. Bleeding me dry, he is."

"What's his name?" Willie asked, almost too afraid to ask.

"Reuben something or other. Reuben Desky, Reuben Dela something like that!" Polchet waived his arm as if to dismiss the topic. Madison drew her breath in and when the others turned to look what was wrong, she was very pale.

"All right, then, thank you Mr. Polchet. It was nice talking to you," Willie said and they all rose from their chairs.

"Don't be daft! It's not nice talking to me because I'm not nice!" Polchet retorted. Once again his face softened and he leaned forward, "But we have chocolate cake on Sunday. You come back then. Sunday. Don't forget."

"We won't," Willie nodded. "Come on, let's get out of here."

The four of them hurried outside. Hurried away from the crazed maniac that couldn't decide whether he was in the past or the present, away from the staring faces of all those old people that had been abandoned by their families and had forgotten what a young person looked like.

"Oh Lord! I couldn't stand another minute in there!" Madison cried, taking in a deep breath of fresh crisp winter air.

"Come on, let's sit here for a minute," Zola said. They all went to sit down on an outside bench that had cleared of snow in the hot sun.

"What do you make of that? What was all that about, Madison? You looked white as a ghost yourself back there," Willie asked.

"Reuben Delasky. He's law partners with my dad!" she whispered, still shocked by the news.

"Your dad? Then it's no coincidence that he rented this place for you and your mom to come to, is it?" Willie asked.

"It seems not," Madison murmured.

"Does your dad know a guy by the name of Bradford Sterling?" Willie asked.

"Of course. He's the man who really helped my dad a lot. He's over the house all the time," Madison said. "Why?"

"No reason. Just curious," Willie shrugged. "So are we going back to your house?"

"Of course. Now that we know he is still the owner and rents it out there's no reason to waste time at the deeds office, is there?" Madison stated. She stood abruptly and started for the car. "Well," she turned to the others, "are you coming or not?"

"Of course," Zola joined her, leaving the boys to follow behind. Willie hesitated for a few moments before turning to Kurt saying,

"Are you thinking what I'm thinking?"

"No, haven't a clue," Kurt replied.

"That Reuben guy. He's not only Tobias's lawyer he's also a partner with Madison's dad. *And* not only do they know my grandfather Bradford Sterling, they are good friends going way back and he's always over their house. Certainly not a coincidence is it," Willie stated.

"Well, as Sherlock Holmes used to say, I don't believe in coincidence. And if we go through all of the questions and answer all of them, then the one that is the most obvious is most likely the truth," Kurt said.

"I don't think that's quite how Sherlock Holmes put it, but I get what you mean. You are saying they are all in on it," Willie said.

"Which part?" Kurt asked.

"Certainly there is only one part, and that is to drive Madison's mother crazy. Else why would they rent a supposed haunted house for her?"

"But what does your grandfather have to do with that?"

"I don't know. Maybe nothing. I just can't stand the guy. Not after how he talked to my mom and how he treated her. I guess I wish he had something to do with it, so we had a really good excuse to lock him in a cell so he'll never see the light of day again!" Willie said angrily.

"Wow! Hate the guy much?"

"Do you blame me? You heard everything today. What would you do if that happened to your mom?"

"Don't even have to ask. I'd do the same thing you did but I'd probably do worse."

"See what I mean? Now how does that demand forgiveness? Like I told my mom, maybe in a hundred years."

"Look, don't go getting mad about that all over again. He's gone and hopefully for good. Why don't we concentrate on Madison's problem."

"You're right. But there is something I don't understand."

"What is that?"

"Madison said her mom is seeing a dark shadow hanging around in her room, she's hearing a baby crying and even Madison said she hears whispers and a baby crying."

"So?"

"Well, when we were in that old library we heard whispers, we heard humming and a baby crying and some pretty loud screaming, but when we asked the girls about it, they said they didn't hear a thing."

"I know, that was strange. But maybe it's like Zola said. There's something going on there, but obviously, one thing is conflicting with the other and that's why she's not able to get a good reading on it."

"Really? Are we going there?"

"Come on, Will, geez. You can't dismiss the fact that she is sensitive to stuff. She said that something is wrong in that house."

"Well any idiot can tell there's something wrong in that house!" Willie cried throwing his hands in the air.

"Okay, so you're a skeptic. But you can't discount what we saw in that stairwell. You can't discount the eerie way that door locked and unlocked on us. You can't discount the strange whisperings and baby crying stuff that we both heard, unless you want to lie to me *and* yourself that you didn't hear it!"

"Are you boys coming or not!" shouted Madison from the car.

"Yeah, yeah," Willie waved her quiet. "Give us a couple of minutes! Okay then. Let's get back to the issue at hand. I still think someone is trying to drive Madison's mom nuts. What other explanation can there be if we are actually looking for a logical one, I mean," Willie sniggered at Kurt.

"Smarty! Okay let's drop the other for a minute, then the question is, why? I mean why do they want to drive her insane?" Kurt asked. "And who exactly are 'they'?"

"As usual. the motive is most likely money," Willie said.

"Hey! You guys coming or what?" Madison shouted from the car again.

"We're coming, hold your horses!" Kurt shouted back. "All right then. So let's agree that is the motive."

"Right."

"And we have to find out who."

"Right."

"*Guys!*"

"Coming! Coming! Geez, let's go before she drives *us* nuts!"

Chapter Twelve

By the time they returned to Towering Pines Manor, it was already late. Each of them called home to ask if it would be all right to stay for supper at Madison's. Willie's parents were used to these spur of the moment phone calls and along with Kurt's parents, readily agreed. Zola was on for a lot longer and when she returned to Madison's room, she had a jubilant look on her face as if she'd just completed her first hurdle.

"So!" she jumped on the bed and grinned. "What do we do now?"

"I want to see that book you found," Madison said grabbing the backpack.

"I'll get it, don't go digging around in our stuff!" Kurt yanked the backpack out of her hands.

"Touchy, touchy."

"Sorry, but it's our stuff okay? Nobody messes with our stuff. Here is the book." They all gathered around on the bed and opened the book before them. "We already followed the family tree line down but you girls go ahead and take a look and see if you notice anything that may be interesting." Kurt and Willie waited until the girls got to the last page and discovered the torn out photograph.

"So what happened here?" Madison looked up at last, an accusing look in her eye.

"Don't look at us that way. We didn't do it. That's Tobias's mother, the one that he referred to as 'the whore', remember?" Willie said.

"Good grief! They hated her that much they ripped out her picture?" Madison cried.

Zola was quiet. She stared intently at the jagged knife cuts across the page and the shredded edges of photograph that remained behind. She passed her hand over the page, coming to rest on the spot where the woman's image should have been. Her eyes closed and her face grew deathly white. Her chin dropped to her chest and her entire body shuddered as if a wave of cold winter air passed through the room.

"She is sad sitting all alone locked away. She is crying, crying, crying into the darkness where the shadows lurk and frighten her. I…I…can't tell where she is…I can't make out the room…it is no room we've seen…so dark…"

"Zola!" Madison shoved Zola's hand from the portrait and gripped her by the shoulders.

"What! What is going on?" Zola shuddered, then looked about in surprise.

"Don't you remember? Don't you remember what you said?" Madison whispered.

"No, did I say something?"

"You said 'she is frightened, locked in a room we've never seen.' What is that supposed to mean?" Kurt asked. "Hey, you're really cold!" He grabbed the blankets from the chest at the end of the bed and wrapped them around her.

"No, I don't remember anything. I hate when that happens. Sometimes I see things, and when I do it's like I go into this trance or something. I don't remember anything after. My mother says I am like her grandmother, a great seer from the old country."

"Well, you certainly scared the heck out of all of us," Willie said. "So what do we make of this un-remembered information?"

"Well, we can't discount it," Kurt said. "She had her hand right on the spot where the picture should be. She did talk about a 'she' and how she was crying. Didn't you say you hear crying sometimes at night, Madison?"

"Yes, yes I did say that. But it's not just crying, like a woman crying. It's crying like there's a baby, too. Did you see a baby?" she asked Zola.

"I don't remember."

"Oh, that's okay, we remember what you said." Madison turned to the boys. "I think we have to go back to where you found the book."

"Back to the library? You want to go to the library?" Kurt asked.

"I think we should."

"We can go back, but I think you should stay here," Willie began but Madison cut him off.

"I don't think so. My issue, my house, we go!"

"All right! But so help me if either one of you starts screaming or crying or anything we'll never take you along again!"

"Deal." Madison slammed the book shut with a resounding thud. "Hey! What's that?" she pointed at the binding. A tiny bulge appeared that hadn't been noticed before.

"Well, well, well. What do we have here?" Willie grabbed the book and pressed along its spine. "Something in there all right."

Madison dug her small scissors from her manicure set on her night stand. "Here."

"Thanks." Willie gently poked the sharp point of the scissors into the top edge of the book binding, then carefully cut along the ridge. He pushed the lump beneath the spine upwards until it protruded out far enough for him to take hold and gently pull out. A thin piece of paper was wrapped around something, and when Madison's quick hands flew forward to grab hold, Willie jerked it out of her way and glared at her.

"Our investigation! Remember?"

"Okay, okay!" she cried.

Willie set the book down and carefully undid the thin piece of paper. It was old and crinkled but it did not tear.

"A key?" Kurt exclaimed.

"Just a stupid key?" Madison cried, disappointed.

"It's not a stupid key, Madison." Zola touched it and shivered. "It's the key that is *the* key to this whole investigation."

"So, if it is, where do we go now?" Madison asked.

"We'll go back to the library and we'll all look around properly this time. Maybe there's something there that will tell us where this key belongs. Let's go," Willie said.

"Hold on," Madison ran back and retrieved four flashlights. "Can't forget these."

Willie tucked the key in his jeans pocket and led the way followed by the girls. Kurt stayed at the rear. They passed through the locked door that was never really locked and once more were in the hall of the unused wing. "There, that set of double doors."

"Didn't we try those last time we were here?" Zola asked.

"No. We went straight to the end and found the staircase," Kurt said. "This is the library that Willie and I found and the book was in there."

Willie rolled the doors open and everyone waited while Kurt fumbled along the wall. He found a light switch and much to everyone's surprise, the lights came on.

"You would think the power would be shut off on this side of the house. I wonder if it works everywhere!" Zola mused as she walked around the piles of books.

"Everything's covered!" exclaimed Madison. She went to several of the chairs and pulled off the dust sheets, coughing at the clouds of dust that had accumulated there. "Pull them off the shelves would you?" She motioned to everyone in the room. One by one, they pulled down the dust covers and when they were done, shelf after shelf of antique books stared back at them. There were numerous portraits hanging on the walls. Using the book, they could now put a name to the face. In the last portrait, however, the face of the woman had been cut out.

"So, here we are again," murmured Madison.

"Yes. You can see this is almost the same portrait as in the book. That must be Tobias' father and obviously that gaping hole should be his mother. I wonder what happened?" Kurt whispered fingering the jagged gap in the portrait.

"Take a look at these books! Most of them have the old soft leather binding," Willie shown his flashlight along the shelves. "I'll bet these are worth a mint!"

Zola jumped and looked quickly about the room. "Did anyone else hear that?"

"No, hear what?" Kurt looked at Zola, her face was pale, her hands trembling.

"What did you...."

"Shhhh!" Zola whispered.

A cry, frail and soft rose and faded in the distance. "There! Did you hear that?"

"No, you must have ears like a dog, they catch everything!" Kurt cried. "What direction is it coming from?"

"There!" Zola pointed towards the door.

"Wh..what was that?" Willie looked quickly.

"You heard that?" Zola whispered.

"Yes, we all did, this time," Madison whispered back. She inched closer to Zola and they gripped each other's hands.

"Shhh, try to figure out where it's coming from," Willie headed towards the door with Kurt right behind him. They knew where it was coming from. They had been there before. Yet they couldn't exactly tell the girls now because they had never told the girls in the first place, so they led the way and the girls scurried to catch up. They stood in the hall, heads cocked to the side, ears straining for the sound.

It rose again, rising sharply in a wail of pain and agony. Everyone froze when the thumping grew louder. A high pitched scream, sharp and piercing ended abruptly with the last resonating thump. The door leading to the winding stairs seemed to shudder for just an instant and an icy draft permeated the hall.

"There!" Madison croaked. "I'm not going in there!"

"That's where the noise is coming from. That's where we have to go," Willie caught his breath and looked at them all. He took a few tentative steps and tried the skeleton key in the lock but it would not fit. "Guess it doesn't belong here."

Kurt grabbed the door latch and pressed down. It opened easily enough. He pulled the door open and all four of them stared at the winding stairs ahead. There was nothing in the beams of their flashlights that would indicate anything but an empty staircase. Then Madison's light went out. She screamed and grabbed hold of Zola. Then Zola's flashlight went out.

"Well, we still have two left," Willie said.

"We're going back and get some more," Madison offered quickly. She grabbed Zola's hand and Willie's flashlight and they disappeared.

"We should never have brought those girls," Willie muttered to Kurt.

"I know."

"It's probably a good thing we never told them about what happened to us up here."

"Probably," Kurt agreed.

"All that stupid talk back there even got me scared," Willie chuckled.

"I know. Gives you goose bumps even if you know the stuff can't be real, right?"

"Oh, so now you are saying this stuff isn't real?" Willie punched him in the arm.

"No, I'm not saying that, especially after what happened to us in here. But in some respects I think you're right. We have to keep an open mind, Will. We'll work on the premise that there is a logical explanation for all of this until we prove that the illogical is the answer."

"Well, that just doesn't make sense."

[124]

"Course it does. If you think about it, whoever is doing this is really good. Dark shadows in Mrs. Demming's room, crying and banging noises all over the house. They must really want her to lose her mind. Yet on the other hand if what Zola is experiencing leads us in another direction," Kurt shrugged, "then that illogical becomes the logical. Get it?"

Willie leaned against the wall and just refused to be baited into Kurt's verbal trap. "Where the heck are those girls?"

"I can't imagine why anyone would want to do that to another person, can you?" Kurt continued.

"No, but then all you have to do is look at my mom's father. What a jerk. Can you imagine any father talking like that to his own daughter? So what that my mom didn't do what he commanded her to do. She's not his property to keep or throw out if he doesn't want it anymore," Willie said angrily.

"But he did just that. He kicked her out, disowned her, and then he has the nerve to come here and do that stuff to her this morning. He really is a jerk. Sorry," Kurt shrugged when Willie looked up sharply.

"No, you're absolutely right. He really is a jerk. He doesn't deserve to have my mom as a daughter, or me as a grandson. I hope we never see him again."

"About time!" Kurt exclaimed when the girls finally came back.

"We didn't know if we were going to come back. But then we remembered we left you two behind and ..." Zola was saying.

"Thought you might be scared without us!" Madison grinned.

"Funny!" Willie grabbed his light back from her. "Come on. I'll lead, girls. Kurt you bring up the rear. And don't hit this darn door! We don't want to get locked in again!"

"Here," Madison wedged her flashlight between the door and the jamb. "That should stop it even if it happens to try to close behind us."

"Good idea. Let's go."

"Sure is cold in here," Zola shivered.

Willie hesitated for a moment shining his flashlight ahead of him, remembering the white mist that had mysteriously appeared and disappeared. He shivered involuntarily, took a deep breath and began to climb.

They passed the first turn without incident but ahead was turn after turn as they mounted the stairs to the turret that rose out of the building, above the tree tops. The farther up they rose, the colder it got. Zola shivered and Madison pulled her close to her side grateful that she wasn't the only one frightened. But it wasn't the cold that made Zola shiver. She knew what was up there. She knew what it was they were going to find. She wanted to turn and run, but she knew she couldn't. She knew they had to help.

At the top at last they faced the large wooden door with the huge lock. Willie shivered involuntarily. "Well, we're back to this," he said.

"You guys were here before?" Zola asked.

"Sure. The other day when we found the book. We heard that scream we told you about and followed it up here, but that lock was there and we couldn't get in," Willie said.

"And you never said anything?" Madison screeched. They ignored her.

"Looks like the kind of lock you see on those treasure chests," Kurt remarked.

"I don't think there's treasure inside," whispered Zola.

"Try the key, Willie," Madison whispered.

Willie gripped the lock and slipped the key inside. He cast a look at everyone then turned it. They jumped when the lock gave way with a resounding '*click*'.

"Are we all ready?" Willie asked.

Zola nodded and Madison stood still. Kurt said, "Let's go." He pushed the door from Willie's grasp.

The door creaked slowly open. A cold blast of air slammed into them, taking their breath away. The air hung heavy with a lingering sadness that seeped into their very beings.

The room was indeed the tower they noticed visible over the trees on that first day when driving to Madison's house. It was icy cold and eerily dark. All the windows around the room had been boarded shut. Slivers of pale yellow moon light slanted through the cracks where the wood had shrunk with age leaving gaps between.

They crowded together in the doorway, scanning the room with their lights. A bed with bedding crumbled in a heap and covered with cob webs. A bowl and pitcher lay on the floor, the pitcher lying on its side. To one side, leaning against the wall, something covered with a cloth.

Swiftly and soundlessly, Zola swept past them into the room, shivering in the depths of its cold. Her expressionless face soon twisted into an expression of horror and fear. She threw herself upon the bed. The cobwebs and dust blew up around her, surrounding her in the haze of eerie yellow light from the flashlights.

"No, no please, you are wrong!" she threw her hands above her head as if warding off blows. She flung herself back, sliding from the bed and landing on the floor, her screams piercing into every inch of the shadowed darkness. Kurt ran to her side but she thrust him off and began to crawl towards the door. "No! It is not true! I am innocent! Not my baby!"

"Zola! Zola stop!" Kurt grabbed her around the waist and held on tight. She fought and kicked, her screams and cries a pitiful pitch until finally they waned to silence. Zola sagged to the floor, limp and unmoving. Willie and Madison rushed to her side.

"She's breathing heavy, but she seems okay," Willie whispered.

"She's shivering like crazy!" Madison cried. Kurt removed his arms from around Zola and quickly tore off his hoodie, wrapping it around her chilled body.

"What the heck just happened?" Willie cried.

Zola's eyes opened. "She is here. She is trying to tell us something. We must find her," she whispered.

"Find who?" Kurt demanded.

"There's no one here!" shouted Willie, once more shining his flashlight around the dark room.

"She...she needs our help!" Zola whispered. She sat up and leaned against Kurt. He wrapped his arms around her once more.

"Are you all right?" he asked.

"Yes. There...there was a woman locked in here. She is gone now and we must find her," Zola said.

"You guys just stay here." Willie got up and looked around the room. There was nothing under the bed or on the bed other than the crumbled pile of bedding. There was nothing else in the room except the layers of dust and the cobwebs that decorated the darkness.

"I think you might be wrong, Zola. There doesn't look like anyone's been here for years!" he said. "See? I've just checked everywhere!"

"Willie! What's that over there," Madison pointed her light. Hidden behind the cloth was the only one other object in the room. Willie drew the cloth back and saw it was a painted portrait.

"Hey guys, look at this!" He pulled the cloth away and brought the portrait to them into the light. "I wonder if this is Tobias' mother!"

Madison gasped "Oh my God! That's the spitting image of my mom!"

"Oh my God! It is!" Zola's voice trembled.

The boys looked surprised. Kurt said, "I think we should get out of here. Let's take this stuff back to Madison's room and we'd better have some serious conversation!" He helped Zola to her feet and Willie grabbed hold of the portrait.

"I agree."

"Well, I don't want *that* in my room!" Madison cried throwing a stabbing motion at the portrait.

"Okay then, we'll take this to the library." Willie didn't wait for an answer. He grabbed Madison by the hand and pulled her towards the door. He'd had enough of crying girls, strange whispering noises in the dark and Zola's silly trances. He stomped down the stairs making as much noise as possible. When they got to the bottom he was relieved to see that the door was still open. He pushed on leading them into the library. He set the portrait down where they could all see it.

Madison sat next to Zola who was already nestled in the crook of Kurt's arm. "So what is all this supposed to mean?" she cried.

"Don't know, but I can bet you a dollar this is Tobias' mother, the one he called a whore," Willie ventured.

"It is," Zola said quietly. "She was locked in that tower, you know. It's her I've been feeling. It's her that's been trying to tell me something. Everything's being blocked by something else. Some type of interference."

"So that's what happened to her!" Kurt exclaimed. "All that trash talk about her running away with a lover wasn't true!"

"But what does it all mean?" Madison asked again.

"It means that she didn't run away, Madison. It means that she wasn't a whore like Tobias was told. All his life he grew up believing that made up story about his mom and it wasn't true. It means that she was locked up in that tower and it most likely means that she was murdered!" Willie said.

"Murdered! In this house! No wonder it's haunted! No wonder Tobias couldn't stand living here!" Madison cried.

"Maybe he didn't know there was a murder. Maybe his father did and only told Tobias that she ran away with a lover. He made up the story about a lover so no one would ask questions," Willie said.

"But still! Murdered!" Madison cried again.

"And why? I mean, why would he lock his wife away in the first place?" Kurt asked.

"Because he thought she was unfaithful. Remember she cried out, 'I am innocent'!" Zola said.

"Hey! You remember?" Kurt asked.

"I do. How strange. But I also know that there is something else going on here, something not to do with Tobias' mother. Something to do with *your* mother, Madison."

"My mother? Why? Just because that picture looks like her?"

"No, not just that, something else," Zola said.

"What?"

"I don't know. I can't quite place it but I am getting different sensations, different visions. Visions of a beautiful woman who is in trouble, a woman who is locked away and something different to do with your mother, yet the same," Zola tried to explain.

"You're making no sense at all, Zola," Willie said.

"I know and I am sorry, but I think that if we find out what happened to this woman, the woman who haunts this house, we will know what is happening with Madison's mother."

"Now that makes sense," Kurt said. Willie made a face at him. "Well it does. Just cause she's a ghost doesn't mean..."

"Ghost! Now you're getting as weird as these two!" shouted Willie.

"Come on Will, you can't discount what has been happening even if you don't believe in ghosts. Zola does and maybe that's why she's having these visions, these things happen to her. Maybe." He added weakly when he saw the look on Willie's face.

"Weird?" Madison jumped up and her hands flew to her hips. "What do you mean, weird!"

"Oh geez, get off my case," Willie groaned. "This whole situation is getting out of hand. I think we have to take a step back and let it rest for a day or two. We have to go over all the details, everything that has happened and write things down. Then come up with logical explanations for what we can and continue to investigate those things we can't."

"Well, now that's the first intelligent thing you've said so far!" Madison glared at him. "I, for one, am sick and tired of this dark and scary stuff. I'm going to my room and clean up, then we are going to go have something to eat. Then we'll get down to business. Real business, Willie McLeish!" She stomped out of the room dragging Zola with her.

"Girls!" Willie shouted at their retreating backs. Kurt laughed. "Oh shut up!"

Willie's mind was racing and by the time they got to Madison's room, he had already decided that they were leaving.

"Look, Zola, you can come with us, and Richard can drop you off at home first, or you can stay. The choice is yours. But Kurt and I are going home. We still have homework to finish plus our chores." Willie nodded to Kurt, that little twitch of the head sort of nod that had become their nonverbal signal that they needed to talk things over —alone.

"I forgot about all the chores. Thanks for the supper invite, but we really have to get going," he said.

"I guess I'll be going too, then. No sense in having your driver make two trips to town," Zola said .

"Are you sure? Can't you just stay?" Madison pleaded. "I thought we were going to discuss stuff!"

"No I think this is for the best," Zola smiled at her. "I think we all have to gather our own thoughts. It might be best, then we can discuss everything a little more calmly."

"But, but... I don't care if Richard has to make two trips and neither does he. Please stay, Zola. At least for a while. I want to check in on Mom and then there's things.....things I want to talk to you about."

"All right," Zola relinquished. The beseeching tone of Madison's voice, the memory of all that had just happened made Zola realize there were a lot of things she and Madison had to discuss.

"Why don't we make arrangements to get together on Saturday, early, and we'll go over some of this stuff again," Kurt said following Willie down the stairs.

"That's a good idea. Then we'll have all day and not have to worry about interruptions," Willie said.

"Good. We'll meet back here on Saturday, say about nine? I can have Richard pick you all up if you need to."

"Sounds good. Well, goodbye. See you on Saturday." Both boys threw their jackets on and hurried outside. When the door closed behind them and they were alone on the stairs, Kurt said, "Willie, what did you have in mind?"

"We really have chores but besides that, I just had to get out of there. All that stupid talk about whispers and ghosts and Madison freaking out about that picture......man!....I couldn't even think straight anymore."

"So, why don't we take a break from it. Why don't we meet at The Treasure Room and go over everything."

Willie checked his watch. "We still have a good hour before supper is ready. My mom is making something special for me and Dad, after what happened."

"I think it should be the other way around. After all she's been through, you guys should be making supper for her."

"Wish I'd thought of that, but it's too late now. Let's go do some thinking."

Chapter Thirteen

They stomped the snow from their boots before entering the porch. Inside, they removed their jackets and boots and Willie reached for the key behind the small glass jar filled with colored marbles. "It sure was a good thing Mrs. H. left this key here for us and gave us permission to come here anytime we wanted. Otherwise, we would never have been able to get in to help her that day that Missy died."

"I know, hey! She would have probably been crying on the floor all night!" Kurt said. He pushed open the door.

"Hey, Mrs. Hendicott!" Willie shouted stepping in ahead of Kurt. "You home?"

"In the parlor boys!" she shouted back. "Will you be visiting today? I can put on some hot chocolate."

"No," Kurt said poking his head in the parlor. "We were just heading up to The Treasure Room because we have a lot of thinking to do." They inched into the room carefully amidst the feline attack at their stockinged toes.

"I see. I take it that means you do not want to be disturbed?" Mrs. Hendicott peered over her glasses. She set her crochet needle down and held up the small white item she had been working on. "What do you think, Kurt? I am crocheting a baptism gown for your mother for the baby. It's either boy or girl so it's easy to do."

"Wow!" Both boys eyed the delicate crochet stitch of silvery white thread. "My mom is going to love this!" Kurt cried.

"I am glad. I only thought of it last week so I hope it is done in time for her baby shower next week. Mai Su came by and I mentioned it to her. She was so excited. She immediately ran to the shop for me and came back with this lovely yarn, a beautiful pure white with a touch of silver. I've finished the bonnet." Mrs. Hendicott held up the tiny bonnet with long trailing ties.

"Wow!" Kurt picked it up very carefully. "Take a look at this huh? My whole fist fits right in there. Are baby's heads really this small?"

"I think so," Mrs. Hendicott laughed. "If they were any larger, birthing would be more traumatic than it already is!"

"Oh, yeah. I get it," Kurt replied red-faced. He handed the tiny bonnet back.

"So you think you'll be done in time? It's coming up already. Geez that time went by fast," Willie exclaimed. "My mom is giving her the shower you know."

"I know. That's what it said on the invitation," Mrs. Hendicott smiled. "And it is a surprise, so don't let anything slip."

"We've been good so far," Kurt smiled back. "Well, we'd better get going. Lots to think about, see you later."

"I'll be here!"

"Wow, that gown is really beautiful. That Mrs. Hendicott sure is full of surprises isn't she?" Willie remarked.

"I guess so. Course I guess when you're as old as she is, and have been through as much as she has, you tend to know a lot about a lot," Kurt said.

Willie closed The Treasure Room door while Kurt went over to sit on a window seat. "So where do we start with this Madison issue."

"At the beginning, I guess. The first issue was that Madison says she hears whispers and strange noises and bangs."

Kurt added, "Course so did we."

"We're talking about Madison's issue remember?"

"Okay already."

"Then we learned about her mom's problem after having the baby and her depression and how her dad moved just Madison and her mom down here to a haunted house. I think that's the first issue. Second, do you think he knew the house was haunted?"

"Course he did. We learned that this guy, Reuben Delasky is Tobias Polchet's attorney and Collin Demming's partner. Course he had to know. Partners talk about their clients, don't they?" Kurt spread out on the window seat and stared at the yellow haze of the street light on the corner

"I guess they do. So if he knew it was haunted then it makes sense that he rented the place on purpose , and for only one purpose, to drive his wife insane."

"That's assuming that he's behind all the antics that are going on at the place," Kurt reminded. "And don't forget, those antics have been going on a lot longer than since Madison and her mom have been there."

"True, very true. Which gives us a more promising case against Madison's dad. And if that were the very reason why he chose Towering Pines Manor to relocate them , then it also stands to reason that he would have the perfect explanation as to why his wife suddenly went on a nut. If she was already going through depression after the baby was born, what better way to throw her over the edge completely than to put her in a haunted mansion."

"Do you think his partner, Reuben, knew anything about that?" Kurt asked.

"I don't know. If he's a friend type of partner, then he knew about Mrs. Demming's problems. He could possibly be behind this whole situation."

"In what way?"

"Well, if him and old man Demming are partners, maybe the situation with Mrs. Demming was wearing on the partnership. Maybe it was causing money problems. You know how some people are about money. Like it's the most important thing on earth. Maybe he hatched this plan to get rid of Mrs. Demming. If they got rid of her, than the strain on the marriage would be gone, the strain on the partnership would be gone. And, you can't discount the fact that he was already the caretaker so to speak, of the manor and had to have known about its history. That might be the reason he suggested it to Demming in the first place."

"So you think the both of them are in on it?" Kurt asked.

"Possibly."

"Okay then, so where does the nurse come in."

"I don't know yet. She seems like she's legit, but she sure is bossy. Maybe she has orders to keep Mrs. Demming sedated, that way whoever it is that is trying to drive her crazy can scare her while she's under the influence of drugs. Pretty easy to manipulate a drugged mind into believing all sorts of crazy stuff," Willie said.

"True, very true. But then again, the nurse might not know about the plot. She just might be following orders herself. So we are back to the reason why. Why would he want to do such a thing, assuming it is a him for sure?" Kurt asked.

"Who else would it be?"

"I don't know, maybe he has another woman and she's the jealous type. That's been known to happen, you know."

"I know. Hey! You know what I just thought of? That night, that first night when we went to the house with Madison? Remember you thought you saw someone running through the woods?" Willie swiveled in the chair, excited with an idea.

"Not thought, I did see someone," Kurt checked him.

"Okay, knew you saw someone. And when we got to the house we were outside when we heard Madison's mom screaming inside. We all ran straight up the stairs and into her mom's bedroom. Remember? The nurse wasn't there right away. She came in a moment later and shoved us aside. Remember?"

"I remember. Madison's mom was standing on the bed screaming like a crazy madwoman! So what?"

"Well, if the nurse's room is next door to Mrs. Demming, it makes sense that she would be the first one to the room. But, she wasn't. But if you think about that secret door we found behind the tapestry, she could have been playing the part of the intruder, escaped through that door after we passed it in the hall, shoved the black cloak and hat in her own room before running back into Mrs. Demming's room. That makes sense, doesn't it?"

"You're right. I wish we would have thought of all that when my dad was there. He could have checked in the nurse's room."

"But like you said, we checked that sitting room," Willie said.

"Yeah.....yeah...." Kurt tapped his head over and over "yeah, but we didn't check Mrs. Demming's room!"

"Sure we did. We looked at her room and the sitting room."

"We looked, Willie, but we didn't actually search! What if there are secret passages in that house? Secret compartments and camouflaged entries and exits like that door? How were we to know it was there from the hall? It looks just like one of those hall panels like the rest of the hall!" Kurt's eyebrows arched with excitement.

"Awesome! I bet that place is full of secret passages! When we get there Saturday, let's make it a point to get in that nurse's room and check it out. Grab a pen and paper and start a list. We don't want to forget to do any of these things."

"Gotcha!" Kurt quickly scribbled number one on the note.

"Hey Willie? I just had an idea. We have to search that whole area no matter what. We have to figure a way to get Mrs. Demming out of her room and we have to do it when the nurse isn't there."

"Didn't Madison say that Saturday mornings the nurse goes into Old Brunswicktown to refill all the prescriptions and do personal shopping? That's the only day everything is open and Madison is home to keep an eye on her mom. We could do it then. Maybe we could get Madison to get her mom out of her room."

"I have a better idea," Kurt sat up abruptly. "We could ask your mom to pay Mrs. Demming a visit. That would get her out of the room."

Willie shot out of the captain's chair as though hit by a bolt of lightning. "Are you nuts! Ask my mom to do that after everything Mrs. Demming has done to her?"

"Well, I just thought…"

"Thought nothing! Don't you realize that Mrs. Demming *used to be* my mom's best friend!"

"I know but…"

"Used to be because of what she did to her!"

"I know but…"

"I mean, she betrayed her, Kurt!"

"I know but…"

"Not to mention she got my dad beat up pretty bad!"

"I know but…"

"I mean bad enough to land him in the hospital, Kurt!"

"I know but…"

"And they had to sneak off to get married just to be left alone!"

"I know but…"

"They lost everything because of that! Geez Kurt are you nuts?"

"No, but I just thought if you explained everything to your mom she might want to help us out, that's all."

"*Me? I* have to explain to my mom?"

"Well, yeah, she's your mom. Look, Willie, your mom is the best chance we have. Wasn't she just saying about forgiving people their past wrongs? Don't you think that the loss of Mrs. Demming's friendship, her best friend, has weighed on her all these years? Don't you think she might want to get things out in the open and be done with it once and for all?"

"Don't you put this on my mom! She's been through enough!"

"Okay, okay," Kurt held up his hands in front of his face in defense. "I just thought it might give them both a fresh start together, that's all."

"Fresh start!" Willie flung himself back into the chair. He glared at Kurt, his face fiery red. "Fresh start! What an idiotic idea!" He flung the chair around, his back to Kurt, and threw his head in his arms on the desk.

Seconds ticking by turned into minutes. Kurt sighed and leaned his head on the glass, watching the fast moving snow clouds that rolled in from the north. He'd pushed Willie too far this time. Maybe he was right. Maybe there were some things in life that didn't need to be prodded forward. Maybe that really was an idiotic idea. He looked at Willie, slumped in the chair over the desk, looking defeated and forlorn. He opened his mouth to say something, but couldn't think of any words that would be right in that situation. He closed his mouth again and went back to staring out the window.

Willie was so angry he couldn't even look at Kurt. He sat there, his forehead feeling like it was glued to the desk top. Taking a deep breath, he let his arms fall to his sides, his fingertips nearly touching the floor, and their argument raced through his head. Idiotic idea, he thought. My poor mom, he thought. What about poor Mrs. Demming being driven slowly insane, he thought. What about Madison? Beautiful Madison , with the copper hair and flawless skin. Madison, who hugged him when she was so grateful for his help, who smelled like heaven and laughed like an angel. Madison, who just might hug him again if…..

"Okay," he took a deep breath and sat upright. "Maybe you're right. Maybe I'll ask."

"Okay, thanks," Kurt mumbled, surprised at Willie's change of heart. "So what is the second thing we have to check?"

"Second, I think just you and I should go back up to that turret room and check it out. I mean really check it out!"

"Back! Up there?"

"Are you scared of that room?" Willie eyed Kurt sideways.

"No, but it's not my most favorite place to be either."

"Okay, mark it down. Second is check out the turret room."

"And," Kurt scribbled the second issue. "We bring some good boots, too. I think we should walk around the entire outside of the house and find out if there's another entrance way in the back, other than those double doors in the sitting room. There were no footprints there, remember? That figure I saw running through the woods had to get in somehow and I'm pretty sure he didn't use the front door," Kurt said.

"Good idea. I'm sure there's another door, too. There's probably several other doors. That place is really huge and there has to be another one out the back, and probably one off the kitchen."

"Course! There has to be. Okay that's number three on the list. I think we should go over the library once more, too," Kurt said.

"Sure, but that's a lot to cover and it may take us more time than we planned. So, I think we should check with our folks about staying at Madison's for the night. We could go on Friday, stay in that unused part of the house and check things out on Saturday."

"It's only a few days until Christmas, Willie, and we still have some shopping to do. Staying there the whole weekend will really mess things up for shopping."

"I know, but we'll be there when the nurse is gone and maybe if my mom decides to come, or not, we can get Madison to get her mom out of the house. Besides, the only one we have left to shop for is Mrs. Hendicott."

"Man!" Kurt groaned. "You know how hard this is going to be to keep those girls away!"

"Who said they were coming with us?"

"Duh!"

"You're right. We'll think of something to keep them busy," Willie said. "And the last thing we have to do is find that cellar door."

"Right! I almost forgot about that!" Kurt wrote excitedly. "I think that is enough for one weekend. You know, Will, I was just wondering?"

"About?"

"Remember Madison said things really changed after her grandfather died? That it really set her mom downhill. I wonder why."

"I remember. So who is her grandfather, what's his name? I'll look them up on the internet."

"Great, let's go talk to Mrs. Hendicott before we leave." Kurt folded the list and put it in his pocket and they headed downstairs.

"Everything get thought out all right?" Mrs. Hendicott said without looking up from her crochet.

"We think so."

"And how is your investigation coming along with the haunted house?"

"Not progressing fast enough. Seems we keep coming up against more issues than we are able to solve," Willie said. He plunked into an arm chair and was immediately assaulted by four cats jumping up and vying for the spot on his lap.

"I see. Anything I can help with?"

"Not unless you remember Tobias Polchet's parents," Kurt groaned.

"Not really. I was such a small child. But if you like, we can go through the scrapbooks in Horace's room. He has hundreds of them. He kept newspaper clippings on just about everything that ever happened here in Fisherman's Haven. He worked at the bank, you know. Knew everyone and everyone's business, that man did."

Kurt stared at Willie, his jaw hanging. "For real? Oh man! Can we? Can we now?"

"Of course."

"Wait a minute! Hold on just a second!" Willie called to Kurt who had bolted from the chair and was already to the stairs. "You are forgetting, we have to get back for supper! We can come back tomorrow because school lets out early for Christmas vacation. We can check it then. I'm sure those newspapers are still going to be there, right Mrs. Hendicott?"

"I am sure, Willie."

"All right then." He rose and started for the door, Kurt's chin hanging to his chest. "Oh stop that. It's not like we're not coming back, you dummy!"

"Is tomorrow going to be a visit day or a think day?" Mrs. Hendicott peered at them over the rims of her glasses.

"Maybe both."

"So you'll have time for hot chocolate? I'll bake something. Mai Su brought me a new recipe called Surprise Squares and they look delicious."

"Great!" Kurt's perked up at the mention of goodies. "So we'll maybe see you tomorrow afternoon for sure! Bye Mrs. Hendicott!"

"Bye boys."

They were tugging on their boots in the porch when Willie nudged Kurt. "Hey, man, how much money you got on you?"

Kurt pulled a bunch of crumbled bills and some change out of his pocket. "Looks like six dollars and eighty-two cents."

Willie counted his pocket money. "I have eight dollars and fifteen cents. Come on. We have fifteen minutes to get to the flower shop before it closes."

He stomped the snow from his boots before entering the kitchen. "Hey Dad! Wow does something ever smell good in here!"

"About time you got home, William," Ian McLeish called from the dining room. "Get washed up and finish setting the table. Your mother is upstairs changing."

"Pork chops and honey yams! And what's this?" Willie poked his nose under the cover of the cake plate."

"Get your nose out of there. Flowers?" Ian smiled when he walked into the kitchen.

"Yeah, I thought after what Mom's been through, we should have cooked *her* supper so I got flowers for her instead." He reached into the cupboard for a vase. "Middle of the table, you think?"

"Lovely. She loves carnations. By the way, son," he gripped Willie's shoulder and turned him around. He searched his face for a moment.

"What's the matter, Dad?"

"Nothing. I was just looking for any signs of when you changed from my little boy to a man. Your mother told me about what happened today. You know I do not condone fighting, William, but I have to agree that today, you were well within your rights to do so."

"So then you aren't mad or anything?"

"Mad? Why should I be mad?" Ian handed Willie the platter of pork chops and grabbed the bowl of yams and plate of biscuits. "You were every inch my Irish son today. I'm proud of you. Oh! Not a word, mind you. Here comes your mother."

"Carnations!" Barbara McLeish squealed with delight. She hugged Ian and planted a kiss on Willie's cheek. "You boys are too much. And you have the table set so let's eat! What a wonderful day!"

They enjoyed the special meal and chatted about everything but the incident. Willie looked happily from his dad to his mom and gave a silent thanks for the two best things in his life.

"Well," Barbara finally pushed away from the table. She eyed the dirty dishes.

"Don't even think about it, Mom. I got this," Willie indicated cleaning up. "You and Dad just go in and enjoy a glass of wine in front of that pretend fireplace we have."

Chapter Fourteen

"So what did your mom say?" Kurt asked on the way to school the next day.

"Nothing. I didn't ask."

"You didn't ask? Why?"

"Because it was a special night, Kurt. She loved the flowers and we laughed and talked over supper like we used to when I was little. When her and Dad went into the living room and were having wine and stuff, I just couldn't bother them. They looked so happy!"

"It's okay. I know what you mean. My mom and dad got into that lovey dovey stuff after we moved here and they found out about the baby. Parents, huh? Who knew?"

They spent the morning trudging from class to class, drumming finger tips against the desktop until that annoyance caught the teachers' attention who put a stop to it in short order. The hands on the clock seemed to get stuck and grudgingly snapped from minute to minute. Finally the bell blasted at noon and they were out the door and down the sidewalk before they could run into Madison and Zola.

They sped to Mrs. Hendicott's, threw their school bags on a nearby rocker in the porch, flung off their jackets and boots and hurried inside. The smell of hot chocolate and something delicious baking followed the multitude of paws that scampered from the open kitchen door.

"Hey, Mrs. Hendicott, we're here!" Willie shouted scooping up Little Santa, who gripped the front of his shirt then climbed to his shoulder. He giggled when the tiny wet, black nose tickled his ear.

"Just in time!" came a voice from the kitchen.

"We'll just go check on that fire in the parlor," Kurt said. They went in, put a few more chunks of wood in the fireplace and were just sitting back on the sofa when Mrs. Hendicott came in carrying a tray.

"So what is it today? Will you be checking out scrapbooks or a think day?" She placed the tray down and handed each of them their mugs. "I don't suppose you two stopped for lunch so I microwaved some of those minnie pizza bites I hear kids like."

"Definitely scrapbook day!" they both cried.

"Oh great!" Willie grinned. "I love these things. What are those?"

"Oh man, these are like s'mores, but better!" Kurt mumbled through a mouthful of chocolate and marshmallow."

"You're supposed to eat the pizza bites first, Kurt," Mrs. Hendicott smiled. "But I'm glad you like them. I changed up the recipe a little, but they did turn out all right."

"Ummm, I should say so!" Willie reached for more, stuffing the dessert treats along with pizza bites into his mouth. "So what about these scrapbooks?"

"Horace was a collector of odd things. He had everything in his Treasure Room of course, but he was always interested in what was going on in the community, too. He would save the newspapers, or sometimes just the important clippings and keep them in a scrapbook. He organized them by year for a while, but when he got older, sometimes things got just a bit muddled."

"So, is it all right if we go up?" Kurt asked downing the last of his hot chocolate.

"Top of the stairs, turn right, two doors down on your left. There's a door in the room off to the right of the bed that leads into his private study. In the coat closet are the scrapbooks. But...." she shouted the 'but' as Willie and Kurt both raced for the stairs. They stopped in mid- stride. "But, please don't make a mess."

"No, we won't Mrs. H. We'll put everything back where we find it!"

"So cool! Just so cool! Can you imagine all the stuff that's hidden away in this house!" Kurt shouted running up the stairs.

They slammed into each other at the landing, each racing to be first into that right turn in the hall. Excitement pulsed through their veins with the anticipation of another cool discovery at Mrs. Hendicott's.

They pushed open the door, a plain wood door with an old fashioned black handle whose latch didn't quite work. The disappointment was daunting.

The large room was as plain and devoid of life, as The Treasure Room was overwhelmed with life. A single bed was precisely placed between two large windows. On the left was a night stand with a small lamp, and a large armoire, a small table and chair near another window. A blanket chest stood at the end of the bed and around to the right, next to the cushioned chair, was the door to Horace's study.

They tread carefully through Horace's room. The only sound was the creaking of old floorboards beneath their stockinged feet. It was a stark and bare room, with no photographs, no memorabilia of any kind at all. The pale taupe wall paper with faded blue diamonds stretched to meet the oak wainscoting that rose from the floor. The faint scent of cigar smoke drifted on the current of air created by their entry.

The door to the study groaned and creaked eerily when they pushed it open. Horace's private study was the opposite of his room. The room itself was twice the size of the bedroom with several large mullioned windows along two walls. Set in between was a double door that opened to a small landing that faced the back of the house overlooking the yard and the keepers cottage. Willie inched his way into the room and pulled the doors open. They both stepped out and peered over

[147]

the railing. The backyard was large and just like the front, the white picket fence surrounded the entire place. The yews and hedges were eerie humps beneath the heavy snow. The boys shivered and realized they were standing stocking feet in several inches of snow. They went back inside and closed the doors against the cold.

A large desk and chair was precisely in the center of the room. An ink blotter, ink well and pens, several leather bound books and several small portraits still rested on its top.

"Look at this!" Kurt picked up one of the small portraits. "This must be Mrs. Hendicott when she was younger with Horace. She looks so pretty doesn't she?"

"She sure is. Her brother is fairly handsome. Look at that one, Kurt. Must be their parents on their wedding day!"

"Wow! She looks a lot like her mom, hey? Her dad looks like the grandfather, Horatio Thumbuckle. Uncanny!"

They set the portraits back and looked around the room. In between the shelves of books were walls decorated with tapestries stitched in bright colors and scenes.

"Wow! Look at this!" Kurt went over and touched the delicate stitching of a hanging tapestry. "There's little plaques beneath them that tell what they are, Will! *The Oseberg*. 800 A.D. Viking Burial Ship, found in Norway. Look at the stuff there!" Kurt cried. "There's the rudder and look here, a stowage crutch where they put the oars when they weren't using them. Look at those oars! So cool!"

"Look at this one, Kurt!" Willie waved him over. "*The Flor de la Mar*. Sank off the Diamond Point of Malaysia. Said to be carrying exotic treasures of gold, precious stones, magical bones of animals and slaves! Holy man! This was a slave ship, Kurt!"

"Look at that thing, hey? Sort of a misnomer putting a red cross on the sails if you're carrying slaved people and bones of animals to use in magic! People were sure stupid back then."

"They weren't stupid, Kurt. They just weren't smart. They didn't have the technology and understanding of things that we have today. That doesn't make them stupid."

"I guess not. But strange, you gotta admit they were strange."

"Hey look at this one! The *Bonhomme Richard*. Oh man! This was a war ship in our fight against the British and it was commanded by John Paul Jones! Wow! 1779, it had 40 guns and six 18-pound cannons. Says here it got it's bowsprit locked with the British enemy ship *Serapis* and they both were lost."

"I wonder who did all these tapestries!" Kurt gazed around the room.

"Probably Horace when he was up here by himself. He was so meticulous at everything he probably wouldn't want anyone else to do it for him." Willie said, looking at the others on the wall until his eyes came to rest on the door to the closet. "Hey, there's the door. We'd better get looking before it gets too late."

"I hope Mrs. Hendicott let's us come up here again. This is so cool! Look at this," Kurt's fingers caressed the rounded copper helmet of ancient divers that sat on a pedestal in one corner. His eyes roamed over to the shelf above it that held a wooden box with a marine chronometer inside, a star globe of only six inches in diameter that showed the main navigational stars and a spy glass. He sighed wistfully at how lucky Horace had been, what great times he must have had.

"She will, come on." Willie pulled the closet door open, stepped back and whistled. The closet had been converted and shelves lined the walls from floor to ceiling, packed with books and papers right to the top.

"Well, we might as well pull them all out and go through them as we put them away," Willie shrugged.

"Shelf by shelf, else we'll be overwhelmed," Kurt reached for a book to his left. "Look, he has them dated. This shouldn't take too long then. The newer ones must be near the bottom shelves and the older stuff at the top. Grab one of those chairs so we can stack stuff."

"I want to look at them all," Willie pulled a chair over and reached for the top shelf.

"Don't be stupid. We don't have that kind of time today," Kurt said.

"Boys, phone call. Willie it's your mom!" Mrs. Hendicott shouted up the stairs.

"My mom?" Willie looked horrified and nearly slipped from the chair. "Why would she be calling me here? Oh no! Has to be an emergency!" He bolted from the closet and ran downstairs.

A moment later he came back shaking his head.

"What? What's the matter?" Kurt demanded.

"Wants me to pick up some milk on the way home. Man! She nearly gave me a heart attack!" Kurt started laughing. "Shut up! Wait til *you* get that call and it's *your* mom! See how you feel!"

"I know," Kurt wiped tears from his eyes. "But you should have seen your face."

"It's just that I've been worried about my mom ever since her father showed up that day. She was really upset. And I really get worried when my dad is gone to work and we are at school. What if that jerk shows up again?"

"I'm sorry, Willie. I didn't mean to laugh. Course you should worry. That guy was such a jerk. Besides, I don't think your mom would ever let him in the door again, leastwise I hope not. Hey, you know what I've been noticing, some of these go back pretty far."

"You're right! Okay, then let's not pull out what we don't need to look at right now."

"Okay." For the next hour they organized the scrapbooks until there were only five left starting with the turn of the century. There on page 5 of a scrapbook was a newspaper clipping of the marriage of August James Polchet to Mary

Elizabeth Sudbury of Sudbury House. Willie poked Kurt and pointed.

"Looks like she was happy there, doesn't it?" Kurt said. "It's really weird how much she looks like Madison's mom in that photo. What else is there."

"Okay here at the end is a clipping of a birth of Tobias James born to August and Mary. That must be the Tobias we met at the nursing home. Holy cow! This stuff is pretty interesting. We're going to have to come up here more often. There must be tons of stuff in those older scrapbooks about the wars and treasures and stuff."

"So cool!" Kurt cried once more. He chose another scrapbook. "Okay nothing in this one." He replaced it in the closet.

"And nothing in this one," Willie returned another one.

"This one is years later and…..Kurt….Kurt….look here!" Willie poked Kurt again.

"I'm right here you know! You don't have to harpoon me!"

"Clipping! Missing woman, it's dated December 23, 1915. It says Mary Elizabeth Sudbury Polchet, wife of August James Polchet has been reported missing by her husband. Police have searched the grounds and a city wide search is under way. Anyone who has any information or has seen Mrs. Polchet please contact the police."

"So she did go missing!" Kurt whistled. "Look there," he pointed to the continued article several pages later. "Police have information that Mary Elizabeth Polchet previously reported missing, has been witnessed to leave city with lover. Search has been suspended."

"So what Tobias told us is true," Willie said.

"Yes, but that doesn't make it true. If what Zola is telling us is true, then she was locked away in that tower and probably died there," Kurt said. "Old man James Polchet probably told the police that just to shut them up."

"Zola? You think what she said was true?" Willie asked. "Geez Kurt! I know you really like her and everything but to think she can have *visions* or know the past or future —come on —you can't really believe that stuff?"

"Yes I do, Willie. How could she possibly make that up? She's from a foreign country, doesn't even know anybody here. How on earth would she know about what happened in that house! She knew details, Willie. Details! How could she know details! Besides, you saw what happened just like me and Madison, too. How can you still think she's a fraud!"

Willie considered for a moment what Kurt had said and after several minutes, said "I...I never thought of that."

"I'm not just patronizing her, Will. There's something there. She.....she has this gift...or curse...whichever you want to call it, but I believe she is not making this up."

"So we have to take her with us if we want to find the truth, find that cellar and find out what really happened in that house," Willie said.

"I think we have to. She's a part of this whether she wanted to be or not. I know she only came along to help Madison, but this might just be the way to do it. I don't think we have a choice. We have to take the girls with us."

"All right. But we'll have to lay some ground rules, like no screaming or fainting stuff."

"Whatever!"

They began putting scrapbooks away. Willie finally turned squinty eyed to Kurt and asked.

"So.....how did it feel?"

"What feel?"

"How did it feel to hold Zola in your arms?"

"Oh that—good —nice—really nice." Kurt grinned sheepishly.

Willie laughed. "Come on. I have to pick up that milk for my mom and it's getting late and we still have shoveling. And let's get some of that homework done right away so we don't have to worry about it all Christmas vacation."

"We coming back tomorrow?"

"No, we planned on staying at Madison's for the weekend, remember?"

"Right." Kurt looked wistfully at the scrapbooks once more before closing the closet door.

They said goodbye to Mrs. Hendicott, promising to be back Sunday after church to continue looking through the scrapbooks. Gripping the milk, Willie said, "I'll go drop this off and you get started on that snow shoveling. I'll be right back."

There wasn't much and Kurt was nearly done when Willie returned. "Hey listen. My dad is still up in Old Brunswicktown and supper is going to be a little late. Come in for a minute, will you?"

"Sure."

"Hey, Mom," Willie said as they were removing their jackets and boots. "Can we talk to you for a minute?"

"You rat!" Kurt hissed. "You tricked me in here because you're going to ask your mom, aren't you?"

"Yup. I'm not going to be the only rat here. We're partners, remember?"

"Of course. I'm just cleaning up in here, be done in a second," Barbara called from the kitchen.

"Kitchen is okay. We can talk in there." Willie tugged Kurt behind him.

"All right," Barbara put her dishcloth aside and said. "What is on your minds boys?"

"Well, we were thinking about what you said the other day," Kurt began, "about that forgiving stuff and all and we…"

"We were thinking that maybe it might be a good thing if you went to see….your friend…..Mrs. Demming?" Willie scrunched his eyes shut waiting for the reprimand.

"Let me get this straight, after all that has been said, you want *me* to go to see the woman that betrayed me?"

"We just thought…."

"What! What did you *thought*, Willie. That all that betrayal could easily be forgotten? That because the secret of your father's and mine's past is out, that the rest can be forgiven? Like it's supposed to have never happened? How can you ask that of me, Willie?"

"Mom, if you only knew!" Willie pleaded.

"Knew what? Knew what William?" she said almost in tears. Willie cringed. He knew that using his full name meant trouble.

"Oh man, Mrs. M., don't start crying," Kurt moaned. "It's just that Willie and I are helping Madison because we think someone is trying to make her mom go nuts so they can lock her away in a nut house somewhere."

"Yeah, Mom. She had a baby a couple of years ago and got that post pard depression thing and her husband made her and Madison come here. She's hearing voices and seeing things and the nurse keeps giving her drugs. She has nightmares and wakes up screaming and nearly killing herself trying to get away from something that isn't there!"

"What? Oh dear, Will, is that true?" Barbara asked, dabbing at her eyes. She forgot completely about the betrayal as the boys told her about the situation. She crossed the kitchen to sit with them at the counter.

"It's true, Mom. She hasn't seen her little boy Zane for months. Her husband is keeping him in Boston away from her because he told her that she was going nuts from depression and tried to hurt him…."

"Oh no!"

"Yes," Kurt chimed in, "and he made Madison come here with her mom. There's strange noises and haunting stuff going on in that house and we think that someone set up the house, you know like a magic trick or something. We need to get her out of her room so we can search it really good."

"I see. And you want me to swallow my pride and go visit her and lure her out of her room so you can snoop around, is that it?" Barbara McLeish got up and poured a cup of coffee.

She leaned against the counter, staring at the boys waiting for an answer.

"Well, yeah, sure," Kurt shrugged and Willie punched him in the arm.

"I guess you could call it that. But really, you'd be doing us a great big favor, Mom, and maybe yourself. Madison's mom could really use a good friend right now."

"An old friend," Kurt said.

"You boys! The things you get yourselves into, I swear," Barbara moved to the sink and stared out the window. Snowflakes had begun to drift lazily and glittered in a clustered ball around the lamp post. "Don't you think this is something your father should be looking into, Kurt?"

"He is. We called him the other afternoon when we were visiting Madison and her mom had an episode. We found nothing and neither did my dad. That's why we think someone has purposely set out to drive her insane. There has to be some sort of electronic set up in that house, somewhere. And we need to find it. We already cleared it with my dad that if we find anything suspicious, we are going to call him right away. But...."

"You may be right," she said turning from the sink. "It just might be time to put this entire past into the past. Saturday you say?"

"Yes, Saturday morning. The nurse goes to town to fill prescriptions and shop. We thought if you could show up there around ten, maybe have a long lunch, that would be great. Also, we wanted to know if it was all right with you if we stayed at Madison's for Friday and possibly Saturday nights. We want to check out some of the rooms when nobody knows we are there and see if we can find anything that might lead us to who is doing this," Willie said.

"Hey, Mrs. M," Kurt ventured. "Do you know anything about Mrs. Demming's dad? I mean, Madison said that Zane was born and later her grandfather changed his will before he died. That's when her mom began acting strange."

"That is strange. Why would her grandfather's death make her mom act strange, I wonder," Barbara said.

"We were wondering that too, Mom."

"Well, if things go well on Saturday, maybe I can ask….in a subtle way, of course."

"That would be so great. So we can stay over there?" Willie asked.

"I don't see why not, but you had better clear it with your mom first, Kurt."

Willie flew around the counter and threw his arms around his mom. "Mom, you're the best! Come on Kurt, we have to go ask your mom. See you in a little while, Mom! Love you!"

And they were gone.

"Oh my goodness, those boys!" Barbara shook her head.

Chapter Fifteen

Friday morning they changed their minds. The lure of the scrapbooks was just too much to let go. They returned to Mrs. Hendicott's and went over more scrapbooks in Horace's room and found out much more information. They couldn't wait to get with Madison and Zola and discuss the new information and the plan that they had hatched for getting Madison's mom out of her room.

They returned home at noon, staying only long enough to wolf down lunch and sweep away any snow that had fallen and to finish the last of their Christmas vacation assigned homework. Finally, by three-thirty they'd had enough. They pulled on jackets and boots and hurried to the ice cream shop where Zola was already waiting with Madison and the four of them piled into the back seat of the Chrysler 310. After scarfing down the snack prepared by Shelby, the four of them were soon sitting in Madison's room, the girls cross-legged on the bed and the boys sprawled on the floor, the ancestry book spread out before them

"I know," Zola was saying. "It is a good thing my mother understands about the things I see. She helped me to convince my father that you needed my help. He reluctantly agreed , but only after I reminded him that Kurt's father is the sheriff and would drive to the house to check up on us."

"Doesn't he trust you?" Kurt asked.

"It's not that. He is afraid for me."

"Afraid? Afraid of what? Us?" Willie looked up.

"No, you do not understand. Back where we are from, it is difficult to trust anyone, to believe there is good in anyone. My father only worries that I will be all right because he loves me so."

"Well, I guess I can understand that," Madison said.

"Yeah.....me too," Kurt gave Zola a big smile. "Ouch! What was that for?" He turned to Willie who had knuckled him in the ribs. Willie smirked and batted his eye lashes.

"Would you boys stop that!" Madison giggled. "I understand totally. My father loves me too and he loves my mom. That's why he sent us here so my mom could get better. He wanted me to come along with her so she wouldn't be so lonely."

"Hey, Madison," Willie sat up. "Didn't you say that your mom got really depressed once your grandfather died?"

"She sure did. It was only eight months after Zane was born and she was already feeling bad. Once her dad died, she got really bad. She argued a lot with my dad, started having nightmares and screaming in her sleep a lot. She started avoiding anything to do with Zane. I guess I hated coming here, but maybe it was for the best to some degree. Or it would be if this place wasn't haunted and spooky."

"I think we can help with that," Kurt sat up, too. "We found this article in an old newspaper that Elizabeth Polchet was first reported missing and then a witness said they saw her leaving with another man. So that verifies the story that Tobias Polchet told us. Doesn't make it true, just verifies it."

"You think he lied?" Madison asked.

"No, I think he told us the truth as he knew it," Kurt added.

"So do you think she really ran away?" Zola asked. "Then why am I getting all these mixed visions, mixed signals with all of this."

"We didn't say we believed the newspaper story, Zola," Willie said. "What we've managed so far is that this August Polchet was a real nut case and jealous of his wife. We think that he talked himself into believing she was having an affair and locked her in that room upstairs and she died there. Once that happened, he had to report her missing to divert suspicion away from himself. He probably paid someone to tell the police they saw her running away with another man and that's the story he beat into poor Tobias when he was a kid growing up."

"So why all these noises, this whispering and haunting stuff?" Madison asked.

"To keep anyone that lived here away so they wouldn't find out the truth," Kurt said.

"But then why would Tobias rent this place out in the first place?" Madison asked.

"We don't know that yet," Kurt said. "But ..."

"So you think all of it is a hoax?" Madison cried.

"Think so," Willie said.

"But who would do such a thing and why?" Madison cried. "Why after all these years and what difference would it make now if the truth was found out?"

"Well, who do you know that would benefit from keeping this house empty and haunted?"

"No clue," Madison shrugged her shoulders.

"We think that somehow his attorney, that partner of your dad's what's his name?"

"Reuben Delasky, but..."

"Yeah, that Reuben Delasky might have something to do with this. After all he is Tobias' attorney and has power of attorney over his matters, Tobias said that much himself. He could easily have written himself into inheriting this place when old Tobias dies and then he'd have himself a grand manor wouldn't he?" Willie said.

"But why would he be involved in trying to make my mom crazy?" Madison cried.

"We don't know. We think it has something to do with your dad and the business partnership," Kurt said.

"Just wait a minute! You don't think my dad is in on this do you? Why? He wouldn't! He loves my mom!" Madison shrieked.

"What'd I tell you?" Kurt shot a disgusted look in Willie's direction.

"What! What is that stupid look for!" demanded Madison.

"We were saying how you girls go all screaming and crying all the time. You just can't do that when we are investigating stuff. You have to keep an open mind," Willie explained.

"Just because we say stuff doesn't mean we believe it. We have to run through things and get possible scenarios and work from there. Asking those kinds of questions tells us we have to check on Reuben Delasky and find out what he has to gain, if anything, from trying to harm your mom," Kurt explained. "And we have to ask about your dad, because in most cases....." he held up his hand to squelch Madison's protest.... "I said most cases, not all, it's the spouse. We have to ask what your dad has to gain by driving your mom nuts. Do you understand?"

Madison drew back in surprise. Her first reaction had been anger at their insinuation that her dad might be involved. But now that the question was bluntly laid out before her, she shook her head and thought. "I....I don't really know. I know my grandfather told them he made a new will once Zane was born, but I just assumed that was because he wanted to include him in it. Then it wasn't long after that that he died, heart attack I was told. He was old, after all, nearly eighty-eight and was crippled for a long time. He had emphysema from smoking all his life and couldn't go anywhere without his little tank of air and a nurse. So that made sense to me, too. I just didn't understand why my mom took it so hard because it was after that she grew really strange, started withdrawing and arguing with my dad a lot. I mean, my grandfather was old. We knew he was going to die sometime!"

"So it could really be the contents of the will that upset your mom... do you think?" Willie asked.

"I don't know, Willie!" Madison threw her hands in the air. "I never paid much attention to that stuff because it really didn't concern me."

"All right, let that go for the time being. We told you the main reason we are here is to check over the house again. We want to check your mom's room, the nurse's room and go back over all those other rooms in the locked wing," Willie said.

"Why the nurse's room?" Madison asked.

"Because we are going to look for some electronic sensors or things that could create the illusion of a dark shadow, or some tape recording device that could make the whisperings and baby cryings that everyone has been hearing," Kurt said.

"So you *do* think this has nothing to do with the paranormal and spirits and stuff?" Madison asked, glancing to Zola quickly.

Kurt shrugged. "We don't know. We can't discount what happened to Zola the other day in the room up there," he glanced up towards the ceiling, "and all those sensations she has, not to mention the things she knows. We can't discount that all of us have heard the noises, the whisperings and that's why we feel there is something electronic involved here. There has to be something else going on here."

"There is, Kurt, and it has to do with Elizabeth Sudbury. She is here in this house. I know it," Zola insisted.

"Well she can't possibly be alive after all these years. Geez!" Willie exclaimed. "Tobias is nearly ninety years old."

"Exactly, Willie. She really isn't alive. But she's not dead yet either. She can't cross over because of what has been done. The tragedy of her death has to be brought to light so her soul can finally rest in peace," Zola said. "But there's more to it. I think she's trying to warn us of something. Something terrible that is about to happen!"

Willie glared at Zola. He wanted to shout out loud '*What a bunch of bull crap*!', but one look from Kurt shut him up.

Madison looked uneasily from one to the other and swallowed. "Okay then, what's on the agenda for tonight?"

"We are going back to the tower and the library," Kurt said.

"Why?" Zola asked.

"Because."

"Well, that's a stupid answer," Madison pouted.

"Oh well!" Kurt shrugged his shoulders.

"We want to check it over again, make sure we didn't miss anything that might be important," Willie explained. "Then we are going to go over every inch of that tower room again and......"

"Are you nuts! You saw what happened last time! You heard the noises and stuff!" Madison cried. "And look what happened to Zola! We can't let that happen again."

Zola put a hand on Madison's arm. "Madison, I don't mind. If it will help your mother then we must do it, don't you see? Kurt and Willie are right. We have to go over everything again and really keep our heads and study things."

"Key words there. Keep your heads." Willie looked from one to the other. "Once we get started, you both have to understand that no matter what happens, noises, whispering, ghosts, or whatever, I don't want a peep out of either of you. No crying, no screaming, no fainting, none of that stuff, got it?"

"Otherwise, you girls really don't need to come," Kurt interrupted.

"What!" both Madison and Zola cried together. "Of course we are coming!" Madison fished through the nearest drawer and grabbed some flashlights. "Come on. We'll go right now!" and she gripped Zola's hand and stomped out of the room.

"Geez! Girls!" Willie slapped his forehead. "Hold on a minute you two!" he called as Madison and Zola went through the supposed locked door into the closed section of the wing. He shook his head, frustrated at how things were going and reached for the flashlight that Kurt held out to him. "Come on. We might as well follow them."

"We don't have to come," hissed Madison stomping indignantly down the hall and dragging Zola beside her. "We don't have to come, we get hysterical and scream and cry. Those stupid boys! *Oh*! They make me so mad! Who do they think they are, they just think they can tell us… tell *me* what to do in my own home, think they can talk to *me* any which way they want. I'll show them! I'm not afraid! I can make it through this stupid house without being afraid or losing my cool!"

Zola tugged her arm away and stopped. "But Madison, you are frightened. You do get hysterical and scream and cry. You do lose your cool! How can you be upset with Kurt and Willie when they are telling the truth and only want to help?"

Madison whirled on her. "Whose side are you on, anyway?"

"Yours, but don't change the subject. We asked them for help. When they give it, you don't want to listen. Please, Madison. Listen to yourself! We need them and you know it!"

"Well, I….I just…." Madison let out a heavy sigh and finally conceded. "I guess you're right." She looked up to see the boys coming at them through the darkness, their flashlights off at their sides.

"Okay, so what's going on?" Willie asked.

"We…we…ah, we were just waiting here for you. I guess you are right," Madison blushed with the embarrassment of having to apologize even though it was dark and no one could tell. "We really do need to do this all together. We really do need to help each other. And um, well, um, sorry for that back there. I didn't mean to, um, you know, blow up at you. I know you're only trying to help. It's just thinking that my dad or his partner have something to do with this really upsets me. To think that while we were thinking this place was haunted and it's just some stupid nasty trick just to drive someone insane. And for what? This stupid house? For stupid money?"

"Hey, it's all right," Willie put a hand to her shoulder. He felt her start to shake him off, then stopped. "We all have those kinds of times. Come on, let's check out the tower first. And really try not to scream or any of that stuff okay? We really have to keep our cool."

"All right. Thanks, Willie." Madison managed a weak smile.

Kurt pulled the door and once more they barricaded it from closing with a flashlight. They all stopped and stared into the darkness, waiting, listening. There was no eerie mist, no scary noises only a deep biting cold that chilled them to the bone. Willie led once more to the top of the stairs where the door to the tower room had been left open by them the previous visit. "Well, that's where the cold is coming from. No mystery there," Kurt shivered.

"Okay, systematically. Each one of us will take a wall, search up and down and along the floor as we go," Willie whispered.

"What are we looking for?" Madison asked.

"Anything unusual," Kurt said. "You feel anything strange in here now, Zola?"

"No," Zola whispered softly. "It's just a cold, dark room now."

"What'd I tell you?" Willie smirked back. "Let's look."

For the better part of fifteen minutes they slowly searched every inch of all the walls and every inch of floor. Dust covered everything in a thick layer. Cobwebs stirred like shimmering veils in the corners from the wind that whispered through the cracks of the boarded up windows.

"I'll take the bed," Kurt said. He stooped down, but found only dust and spider webs. The mattress was nothing more than a large sewn up cotton bed sheet filled with batting. It was caked with dust, grimy and knotted, and Kurt really didn't want to touch it but he did. He pulled it off the board that acted as the bed spring. He pressed the lumpy clumps of batting but found nothing unusual, nothing hidden inside. He went to the crumpled blanket and sheets that lay at the foot of the bed and began to open them up carefully so as not to disturb the layers of dust that had settled on them. The blanket opened up and there were stains visible on the worn cloth. He shuddered involuntarily and tossed it down, wiping his hands on his jeans. He looked around to see if anyone had noticed, grateful that no one had. He took a deep breath, picked up the sheet by the fingertips and began to unwind it. More stains, dark and mottled, the reddish brown specks flaked off as he pulled the sheet open. "Oh... my... God!" he whispered thickly and dropped the sheet.

"What!" everyone cried and hurried over.

He pointed, his throat suddenly constricted, his voice unable to breach the tightened barrier. He was too thunderstruck, too horrified to speak. There in the middle of the sheet was a tiny white knitted baby bootie, its long pink ties, or what should have been pink ties, lay fused in the mass of reddish brown stain.

"That looks like....." Madison whispered.

"Like blood!" Zola finished for her.

"Blood!" echoed the boys.

"So there *was* a baby!" Madison reached to the bootie, then pulled her hand back quickly.

"This is where he threw her, locked her up. Her and her baby," Zola whispered. Tears slid silently down her pale cheeks.

"What do you suppose happened here?" Madison asked.

"He probably killed them in here," Kurt looked at each of them , his face still paled from the shock of such a heinous deed.

"We have to tell the police! We have to tell your dad, Kurt!" Madison cried.

"Shhhh! You promised to keep calm!" Willie put a finger to his lips. "This happened a hundred years ago. Us going on a nut and calling Kurt's dad at this point isn't going to prove anything. We have to find more evidence."

"He's right, you know," Kurt nodded.

Madison gulped and nodded. Zola gripped Kurt's hand and gave a weak nod of her head.

"Are we all ready to keep going?" Kurt asked. They all agreed. "Good, so we'll leave all this here so when we finally get enough to go to my dad with, it will show him, convince him more than we ever could." They nodded.

"And don't forget the portrait we brought down to the library," Willie said. "We have to tell him that was here, too." They all nodded again.

"Come on then," Kurt urged Zola towards the door. She was pale and cold and her whole body was shaking. "Let's check out that library."

This time they closed the door to the tower room and immediately the cold air that had been blowing through the cracks of the boards was stifled. They made their way down the spiraled stairs, each one lost in his own thoughts. No one said a word as Willie retrieved his flashlight and closed the door to the stairs.

They slid back the doors of the library and walked in. Nothing had changed. It was still dark, still musty, still dusty. Some of the dust covers still remained covering the bookshelves and furniture where they hadn't finished from their previous visit due to the spooky sounds they'd heard. They took the time now to remove all of them and put them all in a single pile in one corner of the room. Kurt, Zola and Madison searched the bookshelves and Willie started at the desk. The drawers were tight and he had to tug them open, but they were only filled with more books. He took each one out in turn, shook them by their covers and after finding nothing, placed them back in and slammed the drawers shut.

Zola started on a bookcase, stepping past the portrait they had left leaning against it. Something seemed to be drawing her attention away from her search until she finally gave up the bookcase. She went and sat on one of the chairs facing the portrait. She studied the woman there. She was a beautiful woman whose long copper brown hair hung loosely about her shoulders. Her face radiated with love and her smile spoke of a happy and contented person. The dress she wore was of a midnight blue satin and it seemed that every fold, every crease was real. The single diamond pendant around her long, smooth neck draped at her throat.

"Damn!" Willie cursed. "This stupid top drawer is locked!"

"So break it open," Madison came over and gave a tug.

"It isn't yours, you know."

"So what? Break it open anyway. Why would it be locked? There's been nobody here from the family for fifty years. Open the darn thing!" she told him.

"Okay," he said and grabbed the thin silver letter opener that lay on the desk. He poked and twisted, jammed and jiggled until finally the drawer popped open.

"Well, look here!" he whistled.

"What! What do you have?" Kurt hurried over with Zola at his side.

"Absolutely nothing! The blasted thing is as empty as everything else around here!" fumed Willie. Kurt laughed.

"Oh shut up!"

"You should have seen the look on your face! Like there was going to be some hidden treasure there or something!" Kurt dodged a punch to the arm. He went back to the portrait and reached for the corner. "We might as well bring this back to the tower so everything is there for my Dad, *ouch!*" He cried and dropped the portrait, where it fell flat to its face.

"What?" Zola cried. "What happened?"

"It…it …it was hot! How could it feel hot! Felt like it was burning my fingers off!" Kurt exclaimed.

"How stupid is th…hey!" Willie knelt to the floor. "What is that?" Everyone followed. Nailed to the back was a small envelope. "Come on, let's get it to the desk."

Kurt reached a tentative hand to the frame, touched it gingerly with a fingertip, sighed and grabbed the portrait.

"What did you expect! That it was going to *burn* you again?" Willie laughed.

"Oh shut up. It really did do that," Kurt fumbled and Zola reached to help him.

"I believe you. She's trying to tell us something," she whispered.

They laid the portrait down and Willie grabbed the letter opener once more. He pried loose the nails holding the small envelope to the wood. Kurt, Zola and Madison held their breath waiting while he eased the fragile envelope open. "Looks like a notebook of some sorts. Has some scribbled writing in it." Willie lay it on the desk and opened it. Most of the pages were blank, but there were several with the scrawled large print of a child.

"It's a kid's handwriting! Must be Tobias when he was a child," Madison said.

"It is, look here. It says, 'Today Father said Mother is gone. She will not be returning.'" Willie read the large scrawl.

"Flip the page," Madison urged.

"It has been weeks since Mother left," the notebook said. "Father told me today that she has run off with another man. Father said she was a whore. Father said she had been having an affair with another man and ran away with him. I am forbidden to speak of her." Willie turned the page and continued. "There are whispers in the village that Duncan Gilman was her lover." Willie turned the page once more. "It has been six months since Mother left. Father has changed. Father's solicitor arrived today. He brought a portrait that he was petitioned to hold. He felt although Mother was not here, that he should keep his word and deliver Father's gift as she requested for his birthday. It was a portrait of Mother. She had it painted specially for Father's birthday. Father turned white, then became terribly angry. He locked himself in his room for four days saying he was too ill to leave his bed. He locked the portrait in the tower."

"Gilman! Oh no!" Zola slowly turned the portrait over and pointed. "There! There it is! Duncan Gilman, artist. So Elizabeth Sudbury was going to his studio to have her portrait painted for her husband for his birthday and Polchet thought they were having an affair. He must have killed them both before he even knew about the portrait!" She touched the face of Elizabeth Sudbury. Tears threatened to spill and Zola shivered. Madison gripped her hand and held tight as she, too, stared at the portrait.

"What an awful thing to happen. She looks so happy, she looks like my mother did when Zane was born. I wonder if she was pregnant then, she looks so radiant, like my mother."

"He must have killed them both. Else why would he put in the press about having them run away together. He had to come up with something to explain why the both of them disappeared at the same time," Willie said.

"So what did he do with Duncan Gilman's body? And, what did he do with his wife's body?" Kurt asked.

"That's what this whole thing is about," Zola whispered. "We have to find them. Find them and give them rest. Your father has to know the truth. Everyone has to know the truth. That August James Polchet was a murderer!" She began to cry.

"Stop it, Zola. We'll find them. Okay?" Kurt put an arm around her and she leaned her head into his shoulder. Willie winked at him and Kurt mouthed "*Shut up!*"

"We should probably get this portrait back up to the tower so everything is where it should be for your dad," Willie said.

"No!" Madison cried. "No, please, Willie, I don't think I could go back up there any more tonight."

"Me either," Zola sniffled.

Kurt gave that almost imperceptible nod to Willie. Willie said, "Okay, maybe you're both right. This should be safe enough right here. Come on, let's get out of here."

[169]

Chapter Sixteen

It was some time before they ambled down for their supper. They ate in silence, not even a sideways glance between them, then returned to Madison's room. The horrific image of what they had found in the turret room weighed heavily on everyone's mind an air of sadness surrounded them all. The girls lay on the bed looking through the genealogy book of Sudbury House. Kurt went to sit in one of the window seats and was staring out into the night. It was a clear night, the sky a dark blue fading quickly to black with just a smattering of stars. The moon had swelled over the past few days and was shining brightly, illuminating the entire backyard with its three quarter yellow glow. Willie sat beside him.

"I think we are getting closer to finding out what is going on," Willie said. "Remember that first day we were driving here? Kurt saw someone running towards the house through the woods. I think we need to go outside and go all around the house. We have to find the door that he is using to get in. At least, that will tell us how he is getting in."

"What! You actually saw someone all the way back then and you never mentioned it?" Madison bolted upright on the bed.

"We wanted to investigate further and be sure before we said anything," Willie explained.

"Investigate further? Didn't you think I had a right to know?"

"No, because we knew you'd be all freaked out if we told you then, just like you are now!" Kurt shouted back at her.

"Well, I'm not freaked out about the incident, okay, maybe just a little, but I really am mad I wasn't told right away."

"Look at your reaction now," Willie said to her. "Can you blame us for not wanting to say anything then? We didn't want to frighten you anymore than you already were. We only had your best interests at heart, you know."

Madison relaxed and considered what Kurt and Willie were saying. Finally she said, "All right, what do you want us to do?"

"Well, you can either stay here or if you both decide to come, you have to promise to do what we say."

"Why? Why do we have to follow orders from you?" she demanded slamming the book shut and jumping from the bed.

"First off, this is a real investigation, okay?" Willie jumped from the window seat in front of Madison, an angry square off between the two.

"Second, this could be dangerous. Didn't you ever stop to think that someone really is getting in here to scare your mom? What if we run into him? What are you going to do? Scream and scare him off or stand there with your hands on your hips and melt him away with fumes of anger?" Kurt burst out laughing.

"Shut up, Kurt!" Madison stomped her foot. "I.....I....oh! Boys!" She flung herself back on the bed.

"So what's it going to be?" Willie stomped his foot and planted his hands on his hips, mocking Madison.

Madison threw a pillow at him and started to laugh. "Do I really look that silly?"

"Really!" Both Kurt and Willie exclaimed.

"Okay, I get it. You win. We'll listen. But we are coming, right Zola?"

"Right."

"Then let's go. Boots and jackets," Kurt said.

It was half past eight when they stepped out the front doors. It was a cold, crisp evening and the moon shone bright against the darkening sky. The wind blew gentle, but cold, through the soughing pine branches.

"This way," Willie said. They set off to the left which took them past the glass panes of the solarium. Their shadows reflected through the glass, large, grey blobs that shifted and slid along the wall inside. It seemed to Kurt, who was last in the line, that there were more shadows than just their four. He felt stupid doing it, but he looked around just the same.

Willie scrambled over the snowbank at the corner of the house, followed by Madison, who mumbled continuously under her breath, then Zola, then Kurt. They plowed through the nearly knee deep snow and shivered when the wind freshened, tossing the pine branches in the wind. They passed the last pane past the corner of the solarium and just ahead they could see the dark recess of a doorway. "Does anyone recall this door at all?"

"No," Zola said with a shiver.

"Me either. I wonder where it leads to," Madison said.

"Must be the end of that hall downstairs, the one with the locked door," Kurt muttered.

"Look here," Willie bent down , his flashlight on the snow at his feet. "Looks packed down, like someone was here."

"There was and you can follow the trail back to the woods. The tracks are just barely visible after being covered with that snow yesterday, but there's still a slight depression," Zola said.

"Come on, let's see where they go," Willie pushed ahead onto the trail. "Yeah, yeah, it was packed down probably more times than just the once that you saw him, Kurt. There's a little path leading into the woods. See there? The prints are still there, like dimples covered with a smattering of fresh snow, but there just the same."

They trudged through the snow to the end of the trail where the yard ended. They stopped to look about them. From then on the prints passed into the woods. The trees were close here, the snow not as deep, but shadows loomed at every turn and deep black patches hugged the recesses in the soughing pines. Willie took a deep breath and led them on. Deeper into the forest, deeper into the thickening trees until they lost the reflecting brilliance of the moon on the snow, their only illumination now was the beams of their flashlights. But the prints were still there, more visible now as deep dark shadows against the whiteness of the thin layer of snow, stretched and exaggerated from repeated use.

The moon disappeared entirely behind a swath of clouds and a howl seeped in agony filled the darkness. They all froze, shivering from the cold blast driven through the trees by a sharp gust of wind. Slowly, the howl faded away and a deathly silence pressed around them.

"Listen!" Zola threw her arms out. "Do you hear it?"

"Hear what?" everyone said in unison.

"That groan?" Willie asked. "I'm sure that was just the wind in the trees."

"Could have been a wild animal," Kurt suggested.

"Shhh! Listen!" Zola whispered.

They stood still, their feet rooted in the snow, their heads craned to listen for something, anything, that Zola had already heard. And then it was there, a whimper drifting towards them in the wind. Kurt moved his light ahead, and just beyond the reach of the beam came a movement so quick, a shadow growing, a mist like a breath that writhed and twisted through the darkness. Fear gripped them and they watched in horror the twisting mist that swelled in the cold night air. It came slowly, gliding over the top of the snow, growing in size until they could see the face. A beautiful face, a laughing smile and excitement in her eyes, her long dark hair flowing behind in the wind, something clutched in her arms.

But as it drew nearer the face began to twist and shrink, the mouth to shrivel and the eyes rotted to empty sockets. The clothes torn and tattered streamed around her and her arms, bony and skeletal reached out, groping ahead of her, reaching and clawing, reaching and twisting, grasping for someone.

She drew closer and a weeping came from the contorted shriveled lips, a weeping not of the woman but of a child, a baby whose pitiful cries rose and fell echoing through the darkness. As the white ghastly face drew upon them, screams poured from the gaping mouth, shrill and horrifying, breaking the silence of the forest, until it was all caught by the wind and lost into shadow.

"*Oh——my——God*!" Madison fell to her knees crushing the fallen flashlight into the snow and threw up. Zola fell down beside her and began to cry. Willie stood rigid, staring at the now empty dark space ahead. There were no tracks in the snow. There was no mist in the air. There was no sound but the whispering of the wind through the tree branches , a wind that had died just as suddenly as it had risen. He swallowed but it did nothing to quench the dryness in his throat. He strained into the darkness but still could not see anything.

Kurt stood rooted to the spot. Every muscle and joint on his body ached and the cold sweat of fear trickled down the middle of his back. He was clenching the flashlight so tight, his fingers had no feeling. Finally he coughed and realized he'd been holding his breath. His chest ached, his ears thudded and his head pounded. He doubled over and coughed some more, nearly gagging.

The clouds moved, releasing the glowing moon once more.

Willie turned to Kurt, his lips moving soundlessly. "I...I...," Willie's tongue was stuck on the roof of his mouth.

"It is all right, Willie. I have never witnessed anything like this in my life," Zola wiped the tears from her face and reached for Madison's hand.

"It's just that I thought you were just, you know, sort of making things up," Willie whispered.

"No, things I see are real."

"I guess so!" Kurt finally exclaimed. "Madison, are you all right?"

"I....I don't know!" Madison moaned. She had fallen to her side clutching her stomach. "Was that for real? Did we just see a...a..ghost?"

"I think so," Willie dropped down beside her, glad for the excuse to hide the shaking in his knees. He pulled her close and wrapped his arms around her shaking body. "It's all right. It's gone. Can you get up and make it back to the house?"

"In a minute. Just let me sit here next to you for a minute longer."

"Not a problem!" Willie grinned.

"You are such a pig!" Madison managed a weak laugh.

"Come here, you," Kurt pulled Zola close. "I think we all need a hug,"

They sat for a long time in silence, staring into the darkness with a dreaded fear of what might still be there. But nothing further happened. Finally, when they could stand the cold no longer, they rose, and holding hands, they walked back towards the house, somehow knowing that what happened back there in the trees was over and that no one on earth was ever going to believe them.

They retraced their tracks to the back door. When Willie turned the handle they found that it was not locked. "Well, anyone could get in here. We'd better lock it on the inside."

"Good idea. Whoever is coming in this way won't be able to get in again," Madison said. As soon as they were all in she turned and snapped the deadbolt. "There!"

"Unless whoever it is has a key," Kurt added.

"And then we'll know for sure it is a real live human person doing this, won't we?" Willie said. "Come on, let's see where this leads to." They went forward through another short hall. To their left were the zigzag features of stairs going up.

"I'll bet those are the stairs we went up from the solarium to the second floor."

"Looks like," Kurt tried a door to their right. "Another set of stairs. Man! This place is full of stairs!"

"These old mansions used to employ lots of servants," Madison said, "so those stairs probably go to the servants' quarters. You can reach them from every part of the house I guess."

"We'll check them out later if we need to," Willie said playing his flashlight down the dark hallway.

"This is the downstairs hall to the rooms to the part of the house we are not using," Madison said. She ran her hand along the wall on her left. "And this wall must be the wall adjacent to the solarium."

"And this must be their utility room," Zola said shining her light into the next room.

Kurt said, "Mrs. Hendicott said that was added at a later date. I wonder how we get back into the solarium."

"Hey guys!" Zola called from behind them. "Doesn't this look a bit odd to you?"

The three of them went down to inspect the zigzag of upstairs. After a moment Willie said,"Not seeing anything."

"Look close. If you count the stairs, there's at least five steps before the wall starts here." She pointed.

"So? What's that supposed to mean?" Madison asked.

"If the door to the solarium is at the foot of the stairs on the other side like you guys said, then why does the wall start in so far? Wouldn't you think it would be right at the start of the steps, too?"

"Oh, I get it!" Kurt cried. "There's a false wall there! So let's start banging on that wall. There has to be a secret door or an opening there somewhere. You and Madison start at that end, me and Zola will start here."

For several minutes they knocked and tapped from floor to as high as they could reach towards the ceiling. But there was nothing. No secret panel. No hidden door. They met in the middle of the hall and sat on the floor, disappointed.

"Now what?" Kurt asked.

"Well, it was worth a try," Madison shrugged. "Maybe it doesn't exist. The cellar I mean."

"Oh, it exists all right. Mrs. Hendicott said so and Tobias was pretty nervous telling us about it," Willie said.

"Oh, I forgot about Tobias," Madison said with a shiver.

Kurt ran the beam of the flashlight up and down the hall. "That's a pretty neat design on the wall, though. I like the way they laid out the crisscross on the wood trim and those big round wood things in the middle. Hey!" He jumped up and once more went along the wall pressing those big round wood things until he reached the third one from the stairs. It gave way beneath the pressure of his finger and the entire panel of wall drew inward. "Ugh!" he coughed.

Willie, Madison and Zola shivered behind him when a blast of musty cold air gushed from the opening.

"Looks like we found the cellar!" Willie mumbled from behind his sleeve.

Kurt pushed the flashlight beneath his chin and made a face, turned to them and said, "We going down?"

"Oh Kurt stop that, you idiot! This place is scary enough!" Madison slapped his shoulder.

"Sorry, had to. I'll lead this time." Kurt stepped inside onto a small landing, the grin slowly fading from his face when he looked about. To the right was a set of old wooden stairs that were covered in dust and cobwebs. They ended in a shroud of darkness at the bottom. "Looks like nobody has been down here since poor Tobias was locked in!"

"Don't tell us that! He said he…."

"Quiet, Madison, let's just go down," Willie said.

"Careful, some of these are pretty old and rickety and there's no rail. Stay close," Kurt started down testing each step as he went. The old wood creaked, groaned and sagged but finally they arrived at the bottom.

[178]

Chapter Seventeen

The cellar was dark and permeated with the dank malodorous smell of age and neglect. The floor, once covered with paving stones , was broken and heaved up where water seeped in and out with the winter thaws. The walls were of mortared stone, large round rocks coursed row upon row, the chinking mortar in between cracking and falling, leaving gaps between them. Once at the bottom of the stairs, they saw that there were several rooms that branched from the main section. The first one they entered to their right was lined with shelves and some of them still held jars of fruits and vegetables that were probably a hundred years old or more. "Must be their canning storage room," Zola whispered.

The second room, much larger than the first, contained a heavy wood table in the center, several large hooks hanging from the ceiling at one end and a chipped marble sink. Large knives and saws lay beneath the dust on the table. "Oh man!" Willie groaned. "Let's get out of here."

"Why? What is this room?" Madison asked.

"It's the slaughter room. You know, where they brought their animals to be cut up and cured for their food." Willie put his arm across his face once more. "They'd hang them on those hooks, drain the blood and..."

"Oh yuk! Why did you have to tell me that? That's so disgusting!" Madison shrank towards the door.

"Well, that's how things were done, you know? And besides, we have to face the possibility that August Polchet maybe murdered his wife in this room," Kurt said grimly.

"Now   that really is disgusting!" Madison cried. She grabbed Zola's hand and hurried out.

"Never would have thought of that, Kurt."   Willie whispered while he searched the rest of the room. "There's no human bones here but that doesn't mean anything either."

"Come on, girls are freaking out there all alone," Kurt grinned at Willie.

They continued their search. The main area of the cellar was   curved at one end where a large oval room   held a furnace. Next to that was an open   entry room covered in lumpy layers and black dust.

"Must be the old furnace. Way back in the day I guess they used to burn coal and this big whale of a thing was the burner. That room there would have been the coal storage, look there," Willie pointed to a boarded up hole in the wall. "That was probably where they shoveled the coal in here that's why it's so black. Don't touch it!" he warned Madison. "That stuff is really hard to get off, trust me, I know."

"How do you know so much about this stuff, Willie?" Zola asked.

"My dad talks a lot about mining and the different methods and the olden days. Never about *his* past but a lot about *the* past."

"He's pretty smart, to know so much about so many things," Zola said.

"I know, he sure is," Willie said proudly.

"So what happens now,   there's no more rooms down here. This must be the outside wall." Kurt patted several of the round rocks and ran his flashlight around the cellar once more. "We might as well go, doesn't look like any more to see down here." They started towards the stairs.

But something was troubling Madison. She turned and ran her flashlight along the wall behind her.

"What's wrong?" Zola asked.

"Don't you think it's strange that there are no rooms on that whole front wall?" Madison asked. "Shouldn't that hole for the coal in that room there mean there's something else along here?" The boys stopped and stared at her. "I mean, why have all this space and no rooms on that side but the coal room?"

"That's probably just how it was built. We may be under the solarium and this would be the end of the house," Kurt said.

"I don't think so, Kurt. Remember Mrs. Hendicott said the solarium was added later. That would mean it would be further that way," Willie indicated past the wall.

"So you think they didn't extend the cellar when they built the solarium?" Kurt asked.

"I don't know," Willie shrugged. "But I think we'd better get out of h...."

They all froze when the boards on the stairs behind them creaked. One by one the old steps groaned as if from a weight ...as if from pressure...as if from footsteps. They looked up, but no one was there.

And then the whimpering started. The muffled whimpering of a baby, soft and muted, as though just stretching from sleep and beginning to wake, was heard. It came and was gone and came again through the very walls, absorbed by the very soul of the house that cried out for help.

A mist rose on the stairs in front of them and a bleak skull stared at Kurt, Willie, Madison and Zola. Sunken eyes, black and hollow in a white ghostly face, seemed frail and fading. The mist floated across the open space, down the stairs and disappeared into the wall.

"Whew!" Kurt wiped sweat from his forehead. He grabbed Zola's hand and started for the stairs. "Let's get...."

Knocking! Banging and knocking and scratching as though something or someone were clawing to get out. A scrape and a smack, scrape and a smack, always a scrape and a smack as the pitched cries of a woman broke over them. A scrape and a smack and then the muted moans and the fading cries of the baby and all was silent.

[181]

Zola clung to Kurt. "She's here!"

"Huh?" Kurt and Willie said together, flashlights flinging from corner to corner around the room.

"She's here. She's telling us not to go, to keep looking."

"What are we looking for?" Madison whispered. She crept closer to Zola and peered around.

"For her. For Elizabeth. Where are you Elizabeth!" Zola whispered stepping into the center of the space and looking around with her flashlight. "Help us, Elizabeth. Show us where you are!"

A muted cry. And silence.

"Elizabeth!" Zola moved around the room, her ear pressed to the very stones of the cellar walls, her fingertips probing, searching. "Elizabeth! Help me find you."

"Good Lord, I would never do that!" Madison shrank behind the boys.

Another cry. A baby's whimper.

"Zola! Zola don't move!" Kurt ran to her side. "Look there! Do you see? Do you all see it? The mortar and stones are a different color, like they were added later than the rest of the cellar walls."

"I...I do see it, Kurt," Madison stuttered.

Kurt ran into the butchering room returning with several large knives. "Here!" He thrust one into Willie's hands. "Start digging!"

"What!"

"Start digging. I think we have to dig here!" Kurt jabbed over and over against the mortar, stabbing at the chunks that fell out, digging at the stones to dislodge them. Willie shook his head, then he too, started digging. Madison and Zola stepped carefully in and out removing the fallen debris until, finally, there was a large enough opening where both boys could reach in. They threw their knives down and one to each side of the hole, reached in, grabbed onto the sides and pulled the stones down. They jumped out of the way when they tumbled forward and when the dust cleared all four pointed their flashlights inside.

They saw her then. The skeletal remains lying on shredded clothing, her arms wrapped around the bundle of rotted cloth, holding tight to the small skeleton that remained of her child.

Madison and Zola started to cry. Kurt wanted to turn his head away but his eyes seemed glued to the small bundle of bones clutched in the skeletal arms. Willie stared in shocked disbelief.

"She was telling us all along. That's what the messages were, don't you see?" Zola wiped her face. "When we were up in that turret room, she wanted us to know she had been locked away up there. That's why she slammed the door on us, so we would go all the way up. And when we were in the woods, she thought we were going away and she wanted to turn us back to the house. And just now, she thought we were leaving, that's why she scared us again on those stairs. She thought we were leaving again, she led us to the cellar so we could find her, so we could set her soul to rest."

No one dared speak. They were all too stunned. First the ghost and now the skeleton. It was simply too much to take in. Finally Madison said, "Then, what has all of this to do with my mom?"

"I'm not sure. The visions were mixed and didn't make sense. But now that we've found ...*her*," Zola nodded towards the corpse. "Maybe now they'll make more sense. I just have to think."

"Why don't we get out of this creepy place." Willie rose, pulling Madison up. Kurt did the same, helping Zola to her feet. They started across the room. "I think we'll be able to put a few things together and…."

SLAM!

They all jumped and stared up to the top of the stairs.

"*The door*!" they all shouted and started to run, but they were too late. The door had slammed shut, sealing them in the cellar.

"Check around!" Willie shouted pressing all around the walls. "Check around! There has to be a release mechanism. If we got in, we should be able to get out!"

They searched frantically, nearly shoving each other off the stairs. Finally, after a futile fifteen minutes and many slivers later, they came to a gasping stop and stared at each other. "Nothing! Damn it all!" Willie cursed.

"Willie!" Zola cried.

"Sorry! We should have known that was going to happen!" he moaned.

"But no one knew we were down here!" Madison said. "And if what Zola says is true about her — Elizabeth, leading us here to discover her, she wouldn't be the one locking us down here, would she?"

"Don't be stupid. This was done by a person!" Willie shouted angrily slamming his fist on the locked door.

"Don't call me stupid!" Madison shouted back. "First of all, William McLeish, nobody was around when that first door slammed on us, was there? Second of all, no one was around when that…that…thing attacked us in the forest, was there? Third of all, no one was down here when that….that…that thing showed us where to dig, was there? So don't go calling me stupid when everything that has happened was done by the….the…ghost, spirit, or whatever you want to call it, of Elizabeth!" She set her fists to her hips daring Willie to continue the argument.

"All right already. Maybe that was out of line. I didn't mean to say or imply that you are stupid. I only meant that, like you said, now that Elizabeth has been found, that maybe someone must have seen us. Someone must have followed us. Sorry."

Madison glared at him for a moment before saying, "All right then. Apology accepted."

Kurt shook his head and went to sit down on a step. Zola followed, sitting one above him and Madison one below. Willie stepped between them and sat below Madison.

"Maybe nobody knew we came down here, but maybe the person who's been letting in the intruder came down the hall to let him in again and saw the door open. Maybe that person heard us down here and locked us in. That's the one explanation," Willie said.

"And the other explanation?" Zola asked.

"Maybe the guy who's been getting in found the door locked and used his key to get in. He would have seen the cellar door open, heard us down here and slammed the door to prevent us from getting back up," Willie said.

"But why?" Madison cried. "What has all of this with Elizabeth got to do with my mom? I just don't understand!"

"Madison, think of this," Kurt started. "Now don't go getting all freaky on me okay, I'm just speculating. Think of this. What if whoever it is that's trying to drive your mom crazy knew about this place, knew about this cellar. What if he intended to do the same thing to her that old man Polchet did to his wife? Maybe he intended to lock her up in here. Who would ever have found her? Nobody else knew about this place. We found it by accident. No one would ever think your mom would be locked in here. If she ever turned up missing, they would think she went off her rocker, ran out into the night, into the freezing winter and got lost in the woods and froze to death. They wouldn't find a body til next spring, if they found one at all!"

"Oh, Kurt! That is so horrible!" Madison began to cry. "Why would someone do that to my mom? Why?"

"It's either for this house, or for the money," Willie said.

"Money? What money?" Madison cried.

"The money from your grandfather's will. Didn't you say he changed his will once your little brother Zane was born?"

"Yes but...."

"So what if he changed it to just give the money to you and Zane? What if by getting rid of your mom, and you, all that money would then go to Zane and since he's just a little baby, it wouldn't take much to get rid of him and then the money would ...." Willie stopped when he saw the horror register in Madison's eyes.

"....my dad!" she whispered. "You think it's my dad? Why? He has money? He has his law firm? He has everything...everything! Why?" Madison threw her arms around Willie's neck and sobbed.

"We don't know....we just don't know. We could be wrong....actually we probably are wrong...we can hope we are wrong...." Willie scrunched his face into a 'help me' look at Kurt.

"Well, let's not think about that now. Our first priority is getting out of here. Then I think we are going straight to my dad!" Kurt exclaimed.

"So how do we get out!" Madison cried, her voice quivering. "We have to get out! We have to help my mom! We have to warn her, to get out of here, to hide, to run!"

"I don't know. Don't panic. We'll figure something out okay?" Kurt said, only this time it was his turn to look at Willie for that pleading 'help me' look.

Chapter Eighteen

Saturday morning dawned with a brilliant blue sky. The sun rose with a warmth that began to soften the crusty snow and soon the icicles began to drip. Barbara McLeish sat at the kitchen counter, a cold cup of coffee clutched between the palms of her hands.

"You nursing that cold coffee or would you like a hot refill?" Her husband, Ian said, coming in from the living room.

"Actually, I don't want any at all. I've been sitting here thinking, no, dreading really, going to see Roz again. I know I promised the boys but now that it's time to face the music and actually *go* there, I've been having second thoughts."

"Lovie, you promised the boys, that's one thing. But don't you owe it to yourself to face her with the truth? After all these years it probably has been just as horrible for her as it was for you."

"Oh, Ian! How can you say such things? How can you forget what my father did? The beating you took, the running we had to do?"

"I know, I know, Lovie," Ian pulled her into a warm embrace. "But if I can let it go, why can't you?"

"And my father? Will you let that go, too?" she asked.

Ian pulled away and walked to the sink. "Now that might be a lot more to ask."

"It's the same thing...."

"No...no it isn't, Barb," Ian spun around "No, your father tried to destroy us. Destroy you! I don't think Rozlin had any of that in mind when she was telling him about us. I think she was a pawn, used for the information and she probably felt worse as the betrayer than you ever did as the betrayed!"

"That's it then!" Barbara slammed her palms down on the counter top and rose. "How do I look?"

"You look as if you are about to do battle."

"I just might. I just might. If I'm back in five minutes you'll know how it went." Barbara quickly buttoned up her coat and left before she could change her mind again.

She drove the distance through town, slowly and cautiously. The snow on the road was already turning to a heavy slush that tugged and wrenched the wheels every-which-way. Children were coming out to play, pelting snowballs in the slush, splattering it across the roadway. After what seemed like eons of being pulled to and fro, Barbara slowed to a stop. Ahead was the sign that indicated to her right was the road going south to the freeway and the left to the private drive of Towering Pines Manor. She swallowed, turned the car left and followed the narrow winding drive.

She knocked on the door and waited, tapping her boots, looking anxiously to her left and right hoping no one would answer the door. But someone did.

"Why! Miss Barbara!" Agnes cried. She threw her arms around Barbara's neck and hugged her tight.

"Oh, Agnes! You're still with her!"

"Oh yes, Miss Barbara. I would never leave my Rozlin's side. Come in, come in! She'll be so happy to see you!"

"Will she, Agnes? Will she really?" Barbara frowned at Agnes who took her coat and gloves and nodded.

"I don't know what you know about what's been happening, but I can tell you one thing, Miss Barbara, she's never been the same since that day."

"Neither have I," Barbara said.

"Would you like to come to her room?" Agnes started for the stairs.

"No, I think I should meet her down here. In here." Barbara had been looking around the large hall and spotted the sun shining through the windows of the solarium. "It looks so inviting and warm in there. Do you think she would come down?"

"I can get her down here, don't you worry Miss Barbara," Agnes smiled happily.

"Oh, Agnes! Don't tell her it's me! She might not." But Agnes only smiled back and hurried off.

When Agnes had gone, Barbara walked into the spacious and bright sunlit room. The green foliage of flowering potted plants was everywhere. The gentle trickle of water from the fountain was soothing. She sat at the corner of the room where a large cushioned lounge leaned up against the warmth of the glass. She pressed her hair back into place. She drummed her fingers against her knees, she shifted her position over and over again until she realized she was anxious and nervous – actually frightened was more the way she felt.

"Miss Rozlin, I'll just fetch some tea, shall I?" Barbara could hear Agnes over the soft tread of their approach.

Rozlin Demming entered the solarium leaning heavily on the old woman's shoulder, who stooped to bear the load. She came to a dead stop when she saw Barbara McLeish sitting in front of her.

Barbara jumped up quickly and took a few tentative steps forward. She wasn't sure what Rozlin's reaction would be. She hesitated, but only long enough to hear Rozlin say,

"Oh my God! Barbie!" She released her hold on Agnes and ran across the room, throwing her arms around Barbara's neck, sobbing. "I'm so sorry! I'm so sorry! I'm sorry for everything! For betraying you! For telling your father! For.....oh goodness Barbie I'm so sorry for everything!"

Barbara was taken aback. Of all the possible ways their meeting could have gone, she surely hadn't expected that. She withdrew from Rozlin's arms and said, "Oh Roz, me too!" Then they both began to cry and hug each other. "Come and sit down. Let's leave what happened in the past in the past and start anew."

"Can you truly forgive me?" Rozlin wiped her face on her handkerchief.

"Yes. It wasn't until just this moment when I saw you that I realized how much I've missed you! Missed us!"

"Oh, me too!" Agnes returned with a tray and set it on the table in front of them. She left them with a smile on her face.

"So tell me what's been going on with you all these years?" Barbara said pouring two cups of tea.

"Not much. But how did you know I was here?" Rozlin accepted a cup, tucked her legs beneath her and turned to face Barbara.

"My son, Willie."

"Willie?" Rozlin asked. "Oh! You mean that red-haired boy who was here with Madison? Good grief! I should have known? I should have recognized the very look of Ian on the boy!"

"He's told me you are in some sort of trouble, Roz. Want to tell me about it?"

"I....I hardly know where to begin."

"Beginning always helps," Barbara smiled.

"The beginning is back where we don't want to go, Barbie. You see, it wasn't long after....well after you left...that I found out I was pregnant, too. My father refused to allow scandal and he forced Collin and I to get married. Oh, at first it was all right. We both cared enough about each other to make it friendly those first few years. But then it puttered out. I found I could not forgive what Collin did when he turned traitor on me. Everything I had told him in confidence about you and Ian he was turning around and telling it right to your father."

"So....it wasn't you who told him I was pregnant?" Barbara asked.

"No! I would never! We were like sisters, Barb! Is that what you thought? That all along I had been the one? I would never!"

"Oh Roz, we should have gotten together years ago. Talked this out years ago. All this time….wasted."

"I know. But it's over now, isn't it? We're back aren't we?"

"Absolutely! I'm so glad you're here. We are going to have so much fun together. We'll start with next week. I'm giving a baby shower for a good friend, Marge Brandon. You met her son, Kurt, who is Willie's best friend. His dad is Sheriff Robert Brandon. Marge is such a wonderful friend. You must come!"

"Sounds wonderful."

"It will be now that you're coming. So, now that that's settled, finish your story. Sorry I interrupted."

"That's all right. Where was I? So, I found out later that Collin had betrayed you. And it was all for money, Barbie. Your father promised him a lucrative partnership with one of the largest firms in Boston , and that's why he did it. Once I found that out, our marriage began to fail. Really, I think it was doomed right from the beginning. Oh, we stuck it out together because that's what Father's will stipulated. It said that if we should ever divorce, the entire contents of his will would go to charity. And then, several years ago, Collin came to me and said what fools we'd been all those years wasting our lives pretending when we should really be trying to make it work. He promised he'd change. He promised things would be different and oh! Barbie! I fell for it hook, line and sinker. I soon found myself pregnant again and that's when Zane was born. It was several months later Father took seriously ill and changed his will."

"He changed his will to include Zane?"

"No, he changed his will to leave his entire estate to Madison and Zane! Collin and I were completely out!"

"Oh Roz!"

"I know. For myself I didn't care. I had everything I ever wanted. But Collin was simply furious. And even after Father passed away, all we did was argue. Father left a clause in the will that since Madison and Zane were minors, that I would be the executrix of their estates and manage their money. Collin....well Collin just couldn't see that. He wanted to have control of the money. He said I had been a stupid, brainless woman all my life and who did my father think he was leaving me in charge of anything! Oh Barbie! I was so hurt!"

"I should guess so. It sure doesn't sound like the Collin we all used to hang around together does it?" Barbara said.

"No. He changed so much. I don't think he ever loved me. He was just in it for the money."

"Just how much money are we talking about, Roz?"

"Close to a hundred million dollars. By the time the children are of age, it should be double that what with all the investments and such."

"Whew!" Barbara whistled.

"I know, but I didn't mind. I was getting an executrix fee every year that was sufficient for my needs. It seems the older one gets, the more you realize what truly is important. It just didn't seem to matter so much about the money as long as I had my Zane and Maddie."

"So what is it with this move here?" Barbara finally asked.

"Oh, Barbie. I don't know if I should say! I'm so ashamed!" Rozlin began to cry.

"Oh stop that. The time for crying is over. The time to do something is here, now! And I will help. But you have to tell me first," Barbara said.

"You are such a good friend! After Zane was born, Collin and I began to fight all the time and I was so depressed. I was going through these bouts of anger and sadness and depression. There were days I just stayed in bed all day. I didn't want to see anyone and most of all I was pushing Zane and Madison out of my life. I was so lonely! So afraid. The more Collin and I argued the more depressed I got until I went to a specialist. He said it was nothing more than postpartum depression and some rest and nursing care would see to that. That's when Collin insisted that I come away to some place private, some place secluded and he insisted that Madison come with me so I wouldn't be alone."

"And this is where he sent you?"

"Yes. He said it was a lovely house, large and quiet and private. He said there was a really nice school for Madison, and he hired a private nurse and.....well....here we are!"

"Yes, here you are," Barbara mused.

"I was......" Rozlin stopped and looked about, a frightened look on her face. "Do you hear that?"

"Hear what?"

"That noise. That scraping noise, that thumping noise! Oh God! Barbie. I feel like I'm going insane!"

"Don't be silly, Roz. I don't hear a thing."

"But that's what the problem is, Barbie. This place! This house! Ever since we arrived, I've been hearing things, seeing things. I feel like I'm losing my mind!"

"Let's not get hysterical, Roz. I'm sure there is a logical explanation."

"No, you don't understand..."

Barbara shushed Rozlin and cocked her head to listen. After a moment, she rose and tiptoed around the room. She could hear the noise now, hear the scraping, and somewhere inside the wall she could hear the tapping. "You're not going insane, Roz," she whispered and pointed to the far wall opposite the water fall.

She crept to the wall, her heart pounding. The thumping grew louder and her heart raced. She pressed her ear to the wall, jerking back when thumping footsteps sounded on the other side. She pressed her ear once more.

"Oh, Barbie!" Rozlin had risen and crossed to her, gripping her elbow as if to pull her away from the impending horror.

"Shhh! I hear voices!" Barbara whispered. She tapped the wall three times. Three taps came back. She tapped the wall four times, four taps came back.

"What are you doing?" Rozlin was horrified.

"It...it....it sounds like several different voices...it sounds like a female voice....no now it's a male voice... good grief!" Barbara jumped back. "It sounds like my Willie!"

Rozlin jumped back, gripping her sweater tight about her. "Willie! In there?"

"Willie! Willie is that you in there?" Barbara shouted at the wall.

"Mom! Mom are you there? Are you there in the solarium? We're stuck in here! Hang on! Here comes Kurt. Get away from the wall. He has a big axe and we're going to break through the wall!"

"Quick Roz, get out of the way!" Barbara pulled her back across the room. They stared horrified as the thumping turned into menacing and thunderous crashes and the axe Kurt wielded smashed through the brick wall.

Chapter Nineteen

Willie struggled to open his eyes. When he peered into the darkness, it was a moment before he remembered the cellar. His shoulder ached intolerably and when he tried to move, found he was hampered by a heavy object pressing against him. The weight on his shoulder shifted, sighed and settled back. Madison! He remembered now. Now that he could feel the soft rise and fall of her against him. Could smell the clean fragrance of spring in her hair where her head nestled into his shoulder. She was warm and tiny all curled into the crook of his arm and he, for one moment, wished it would never end.

They had turned off all the flashlights but one in order to conserve the batteries. They must have all fallen asleep and that one flashlight had died. He felt around until his fingers circled around the light Madison held in her lap, her fingers released their hold and he tugged it away. He turned it on and looked around. No! Their situation had not changed. They were still trapped. No! No one had shown up to rescue them. He twisted his left arm from Madison's waist and checked his watch. Nine- thirty! That had to be in the morning! Should he wake them up?

Madison rested against him so peaceful and serene. A sleep she probably hadn't been able to enjoy for weeks! He flashed the light on Kurt and Zola. Zola had slipped down the step to sit side by side with Kurt, her head bent to his chest, his left arm wrapping with his right arm around her, hugging her close, his face resting against the top of her head. Zola's yellow hair, almost luminescent in the glow of the flashlight, shown like a halo where it lay spread upon her shoulders.

"Hey guys!" He called softly so as not to frighten anyone. He nudged Madison who jerked awake. "Shhhh! It's all right."

"Oh dear! We must have all fallen asleep!" she said. "Doesn't seem to have changed our predicament any, does it!" she looked around.

"Um, does anyone know the time?" Zola yawned.

"It's after nine-thirty," Willie said.

"In the morning?" Kurt cried. "Geez! We gotta think of a way out of here!"

"Well duh!" Willie said. "Any ideas?" He ran the flashlight around the room several times. "You guys sit here. I'm going to stretch and take another look around."

"I'll come with you," Kurt rose and stretched.

"Turn on your light, Zola. You boys aren't leaving us in the dark!" Madison said, stretching.

The boys retraced their steps around the room. There was nothing that had changed, nothing that was new. They searched around the old furnace but found nothing, the same with the coal storage room. They were returning to the girls when Willie stopped. He slapped the top of his head and said, "Man are we stupid!"

"Course, you are speaking for yourself, right?" Kurt looked at him. "What? What is it?"

"What? What's going on?" The girls hurried down from the stairs to join them.

"Take a look at this." Willie took his flashlight and panned it around the room. He lingered on the furnace, he lingered longer on the coal room. Then he followed the wall from the coal room back into the large central part of the cellar where they had stepped into from the stairs.

"See what I see?"

"No," Zola said.

"Me either," Madison echoed.

"I do." Kurt walked back to the end of the wall, starting at the opening to the coal room, until he was near the hole they had broken down. "This wall is straight. It leads to the door to the coal room, which goes in beyond this wall. That means that there is another space beyond this room. Beyond.....that." He pointed to the skeletal bodies they'd uncovered.

"That means the door that Mrs. Hendicott was telling us that came *up* from the basement is in there," Willie pointed.

"That means....." said Kurt with a gulp, "that we have to go in.....there!" His light shown on the remains once more.

"Go in there! Are you nuts!" shrieked Madison. "I'm not going in there! Zola tell them! Tell them we're not going in there!"

"They're probably right, Madison. I've been thinking about that door slamming on us last night. Maybe it *was* Elizabeth once more. Maybe there was still more for us to find."

"What else could there be to find!" Madison cried. "I'm not going in there!"

"Don't be afraid, Madison. I'm not afraid. We've found Elizabeth and her baby. She won't be bothering us anymore. But there might be something else she is trying to tell us. What else is there to be afraid of!"

"I...you...we..." Madison looked helplessly from one to the other. "All right. Okay. I guess I'll go. But I'm going to close my eyes until we get past her so someone will have to hold my hand."

"I can do that!" Willie offered.

"You are such a.....thanks...thanks Willie," Madison smiled. She'd been about to lose her temper again only realizing, in that fleeting second, that Kurt and Willie had solved one of the mysteries about the house and had done more for her in the last few days than anyone she'd ever known in her entire life.

"Are we all set then?" Kurt asked. "Let's go." He took Zola's hand and they turned towards the hole. "Okay duck your head and keep your eyes averted. You don't have to look at her. You don't have to be afraid."

"I'm not afraid, Kurt." Zola stopped just inside and stared down at Elizabeth Sudbury Polchet's remains. She bent down and touched the bits of cloth that lay around the body.

"Oh, Zola! Don't!" Madison cried.

"Look here. It's dark blue, dark blue like the dress she was wearing in her photograph. And look there, Kurt!" Zola pointed to the tiny bones Elizabeth held tight to her. The little legs of the infant sprawled from beneath the tattering of a blanket, one little set of bones still covered with a tiny bootie.

"The other bootie!" Kurt whispered. "What kind of awful person would do such a thing to a baby!"

"It's not just Elizabeth and her baby, guys." They all looked up and followed the direction of Willie's flashlight. Flung over a beam in the far corner, were the frayed remnants of a rope that had been chewed by rodents. Beneath that, where the rest of the rope had fallen, was the other frayed end still tied around the neck of a skeleton. It lay slumped against the back wall, the clothes still clinging to the bones.

"Ahhhhh!" screamed Madison and she threw herself into Willie's arms.

"Oh my God!" Zola whispered. "Duncan Gilman!"

"How…how do you know?" Madison said tearfully.

"The clothes. Look at his clothes."

"Looks like Polchet got him down here and hanged him from that rafter. He must have thrown Elizabeth and the baby in here and let them all rot together." Willie peered at the skeleton.

"He killed him then threw Elizabeth in here with her baby?" Madison gasped. "She was alive! She was in here all that while with a dead body until she died herself! Oh how horrible!"

"Look, looking at this and crying about it now isn't going to get us out of here. Besides I think that statute of limitations on murder is over considering that Polchet is also dead." Kurt turned to look around.

"I hope he died a horrible death! I hope it was worse than this!" Madison was crying.

"I don't think there can be anything worse than this, Madison," Zola put her arm around her friend.

"Let's keep going. If there is a staircase, it should be....right....over....got it!" Willie ran forward. "We would have never seen this from over there!" The stairs were enclosed in a wall with just a small opening invisible in the darkness.

They started upwards with Willie tapping each step as he went. By the time they'd reached the top they found themselves on a small landing. There was no door.

"Now what?" Madison asked.

"Well, there was a door here at one time, Mrs. Hendicott said so," Willie said feeling and tapping the wall.

"They probably blocked it in once the solarium was added and they began to use the stairs we found in that hall back there," Kurt said.

"So how do we get out?" Madison asked.

"I don't know." Willie rammed his shoulder against the wall , but it didn't budge.

"Hey. I'm going to go back and see if there's anything else in that slau...that room down there." Kurt started to leave but Madison grabbed his arm and pulled him back.

"Are you nuts! That crazy Polchet guy probably used them to kill other people! He was probably one of those serial killers! Kurt! You can't touch that stuff! It's...it's horrible!"

"I can't think of any other way to get through this wall, can you?" he asked.

"No...no...but..."

"Then let me go. I'll be careful."

"I'll come with you," Zola followed Kurt down.

"Oh, Willie!" Madison hugged him. "Are we ever going to get out of here?"

"Yes, just hang on. We'll cut through this wall and then I think we better get hold of Kurt's dad," Willie was holding her close.

"I agree. It's about time this came to light. It's about time Elizabeth Polchet was proven innocent and she and her baby get properly buried."

"For sure. Oh here they are back already."

"Found this axe lying on the floor. It looks like it should work better than those broken knives," Kurt said. "You'd better step back...."

They all stopped and held their breath when a tapping noise sounded on the wall.

"It's someone on the other side. Someone is tapping the wall."

Three knocks. Willie knocked three times back. Four knocks. Willie knocked four times back. *"Hello!"* he shouted against the wall.

"Hello!" came an answer back. "Willie! Willie is that you?" came a muffled voice through the wall.

"Mom!" Willie shouted. "Mom! We're here. We're stuck in the cellar. Get away from the wall. Kurt is going to try to knock out the wall with an axe. Get out of the way! Go Kurt! Hurry!"

"Okay, but everyone should move back down the stairs. I don't want to accidently hit one of you when I swing this thing. All right?"

Now at a safe distance everyone nodded and Kurt began to chop at the wall.

Chunks of plaster and brick flew in all directions and Kurt kept his eyes squinted nearly shut to avoid having debris fling into them. Willie, Zola and Madison quickly retreated to the bottom of the stairs to get out of the way of the flying debris. After several long minutes they could see a tiny stream of light that filtered into a crack through the wall.

"Kurt!" shouted Sheriff Brandon. "Step back! Step out of the way!"

"Dad! Dad is that you?"

"Yes, Agnes called me right away. Get out of the way. Cliff and I are going to try to ram the wall apart!"

"Okay, Dad. Go ahead!" Kurt gripped the axe and bolted down the stairs with the others. Within seconds a battering ram smashed into the wall sending chunks of concrete, rocks and timbers flying down the stairs. "Okay! It's good! We can get through!"

Madison ran ahead, throwing herself into her mother's arms, followed by Zola. Sheriff Brandon helped them over what remained of the wall. Kurt stepped into the bright solarium and threw his arms around his dad, Willie ran and hugged his mom.

"What the devil are you boys up to!" Brandon cried.

"There's dead people down there!" Madison shrieked and pointed into the hole.

"Dead people?" Cliff Calhoun looked up sharply.

"Dead people. Three of them. And they are in there!" Madison cried.

"All right, just calm down and tell us calmly," Brandon said.

"It's true, Dad. We found the bodies of Elizabeth Sudbury Polchet and her baby and the artist and…"

"They've been dead for over a hundred years but they're still there," Willie said.

"Elizabeth? A baby? A hundred years?" Brandon asked. "What's going on here?"

"Come on, Dad. It's a long story. We'll show you."

"No, you boys stay here, Cliff and I will take a look."

"No, Dad! Willie and I found the truth about what's going on and we need to tell you but…." he nodded towards the girls… "we need to tell you alone."

"I see. Cliff, why don't you take the ladies here to the sitting room and the boys and I will take a look downstairs. Better call forensics…."

"NO!" Both Willie and Kurt shouted together.

"No?"

"Dad, we have stuff to tell you first, okay?"

"Okay. Cliff, to the sitting room, boys come with me." A stream of light shone through the hole and Brandon picked his way around the broken refuse along the stairs until he reached the bottom. The boys followed behind and turned on their flashlights.

"Over here, Dad. Look at this!" He pointed to the skeleton slouched in the corner.

"And look at this!" Willie aimed his light on the skeletal remains of Elizabeth and her baby.

"*Oh.....my....God!*" Sheriff Brandon's voice was strained. "I think you boys have a lot to tell me."

"Well, Madison said there's been lots of noises, voices and stuff going on and her mom's been seeing that shadow. So we followed the clues and we found this," Kurt waved his arm to include the room and its contents.

"We also figured that someone out there is trying to drive Mrs. Demming nuts by using the ghost history of this house. We don't think Mrs. Demming is making this up, Mr. B," Willie said. "Last night someone locked us in here, so now he knows we are on to him. We think he's going to try something tonight. We need to set a trap to catch him. If you call forensics now, it might scare him away."

Sheriff Brandon looked around once more at the grisly scene before him and nodded. "All right boys, we can hold off on the forensics team for a while. Let's head back upstairs. I'm going to have to talk with Mrs. Demming about this."

An hour later, Rozlin Demming had told Sheriff Brandon all about the strange happenings at the manor house and about the changing of her father's will.

"But Mom, it can't possibly be Dad!" Madison cried in tears.

"We don't know that, Madison," Sheriff Brandon said. "But we do need to get to the bottom of this. When will that nurse be back."

"She should be back any time now," Rozlin Demming said.

"Good. We want you to continue with your day like it was any other day. Cliff, you take the cruiser and get it out of sight. You kids, I want you to stay in Madison's room doing what you would normally do, come down for supper like normal, all of that."

"What are you going to do, Dad?"

"Cliff and I will be waiting."

"What about me? Is there anything you want me to do?" Barbara McLeish asked.

"Yes, actually. Here's the plan."

The Hidden Secret of Towering Pines Manor

Chapter Twenty

Disappointed, both Kurt and Willie stood watch at the front door. "Boy, this really is the pits," Kurt grumbled. "We find everything and my dad and Calhoun get to do the fun stuff."

"I know, hey?" Willie agreed. "But at least once they search that nurse's room hopefully they will find evidence linking her to all of this instead of Madison's dad."

"That would be great for Madison and her mom," Kurt agreed. "It's a good thing my dad is in thick with the judge. He pushed that search warrant through as soon as my dad called him."

Upstairs Sheriff Brandon and Deputy Calhoun systematically searched Nurse Winthrop's room. Calhoun was tapping the walls for any indication of a secret passage, but found none. Then he began checking under everything, opening the large bureau drawers while Sheriff Brandon was busy inspecting the closet. "Cliff, take a look at this!" he pointed to a bundle in a far corner.

"It's a black face mask, a black hat all folded up neatly in this black cape." Calhoun poked at the items with a pencil.

"Looks like we found out why nobody ever saw that intruder. It was the nurse!" Brandon said.

"Real neat trick. Go in the dark, scare the wits out of Mrs. Demming, run in the other room and remove the get up, then run back in as the nurse like you were there all the while!" Calhoun shook his head. "So she is in on this. What's that?"

"I heard that. Pull that shoe stand forward a little. I think it came from there."

Both Calhoun and Brandon reached to pull out the four foot high shoe rack that stood against the back wall. It rolled outward and on the back were several narrow shelves containing a tape recorder and a small video camera. A cord ran from the camera along the wall and into a small hole. When Sheriff Brandon moved aside the cord and put his eye to the hole, he was looking directly into Mrs. Demming's room. "Well what do you know? Take a look at this!"

Deputy Calhoun peered through the hole and whistled. "So this is how they are doing it!"

"What a devious and nefarious plot!" Brandon whistled softly. "So the boys were right. Someone is trying to drive Mrs. Demming crazy and it looks like the nurse is in this up to her eyeballs. I wonder who she is really answering to."

"She checked out clean when Shawnda ran her background for us earlier today. She's swinging by with the signed search warrant as soon as the paper work is done. So the way I see it, we have two choices. One is Collin Demming. He might be paying her off to scare his wife. She may not know the rest of his plan." Deputy Calhoun grunted and helped push the shoe rack back into place. He looked around to be sure everything else was left as they had found it. "Then again, it could be the partner, Reuben Delasky. He might be trying to keep everyone out of here so he can gain control and ownership of the manor like the boys surmised, for what reason remains unknown at this time."

"But that still doesn't explain why he would do this to Mrs. Demming. He would still have to have a connection with Collin Demming."

"Not necessarily. It could be for the ownership of the manor. It could be for money from the partnership, or it could be that he has loved Rozlin Demming and feels if he can't have her no one will."

"All right, two suspects. Two great motives and both have ample opportunity and means of getting in here to accomplish their mission."

"Dad!" Kurt rushed breathless into the room. "She's coming!"

"We're done here. You and Willie get back into Madison's room with the girls. Cliff and I will take our hiding places. It's going to be a long wait, but it will definitely be worth it."

Madison was sitting on one of the window seats staring out the window, her knees pulled tight up to her chest, her arms wrapped around them. Tears slid down her cheeks and Zola sat next to her, looking helpless. They both jumped when the boys burst in, slamming the door shut behind them. "The nurse is coming!" Willie said breathless.

"Man! I hate that woman! She won't even let me spend time with my own mom!" Madison said angrily, wiping her face.

"Don't worry. It'll be over soon, just like you said," Willie said.

"Did your dad find anything in her room?" Madison asked

"Don't know," Kurt shrugged. "He didn't have time to tell us anything. But by the look on his face, I'd bet that he found a lot. It might be that nurse all along."

"So it is the nurse? She's trying to drive my mom crazy? Why?" Madison cried "I hope they get her!"

"Shhhhh! Keep your voice down. We know she's involved but she's not doing this alone."

"Some Christmas this turned out to be!" Madison began to cry all over again. "Big deal that there's a tree downstairs. Big deal that we have tons of presents. All of that doesn't mean a thing does it? I mean, look what all that money has bought my mom! Sadness and insanity! She has spent the last year of her life thinking there's something wrong with her, never being able to see Zane or hold him in her arms, having nightmares that no one would believe when she tried to tell them. Oh God! And the worst of all is me! I never believed her either! I am the most horrible daughter!" Madison grabbed for a handful of tissues.

"Oh stop that! What are you looking for, a pity party?" Kurt said with disdain. "Your mom is the one that's the victim here. You had no idea what was going on and when you finally realized that something was really wrong, you had the courage to ask someone for help. So stop beating yourself up over this. Right now we have to keep our wits and help my dad. If this goes down like he thinks it will, he is going to need us to be alert and help catch whoever really is the mastermind about this whole situation. We can't do that if you keep whining and feeling sorry for yourself."

"Oh brother, who would be calling me now?" Madison wiped her tears and reached for the phone. "Doesn't look like a number I know. Hello?" she listened for a moment and handed the phone to Kurt. "It's for you."

"Me?"

"Yes! Take it!" Madison thrust the phone in his hand.

"Hello?" Kurt said.

"Kurt? Kurt is that you?" the voice on the other end sounded tired.

"Mom! Mom why are you calling me here?"

"Honey, you gave your father the number, remember? Is your father there? I called the station but they said he couldn't be reached. What's going on?"

"He's busy, Mom, and he can't come to the phone."

"Oh, honey, this is pretty urgent. I'm in the hospital. Seems the baby is going to be a little earlier than we expected," Margaret Brandon groaned when a pain seered through her belly.

"Mom! Are you all right?"

"Yes.....yes, honey, I'm all right. It's just that....well, I know your father is busy so just give him the message when you can. I called Deputy Shawnda and she brought me here safely."

"Geez, I can't bust in on him now, Mom. I'll tell him as soon as I can, all right?"

"All right. Is everything all right there?"

"Yes, everything is all right. We're all fine. Love you Mom!"

"Love you too, honey. Gotta go. Another pain! Bye!" The phone disconnected. Kurt stared at the silent cell phone.

"What's the matter, Kurt?" Willie asked.

"Mom! She's in the hospital. The baby!" Kurt looked panic stricken.

"She'll be all right. We can't interrupt your dad now!" Madison cried.

"No...I mean no we can't and yes I know she'll be all right. It's just that......the baby....all these months and now it's going to happen! It's too early. Nearly three weeks ahead of schedule!" Kurt moaned.

"No, that's not how it works, Kurt. Babies come when babies are going to come. Isn't it so sweet? She's going to be a Christmas baby," Zola smiled cheerily.

"How do you know it's a she?" Kurt asked.

"Just do," Zola smiled dreamily.

"Well, at least there's going to be one good thing happening out of this whole mess," Madison wiped her face once more.

"No, two. We're going to get your mom out of this mess and get you and her and Zane back together again," Willie smiled at Madison.

"Look, we'd better act like normal, like your dad said. Come on, let's go down and have something to eat. Then we can come back up here and turn up the music so that stupid nurse doesn't think we're on to her."

"Great idea." They all agreed.

Eating and listening to music only went so far to quell the anxious anticipation of the four of them. Kurt began to pace and Willie drummed his fingers incessantly on the window ledge. Finally Madison tugged them all into her mom's room and they played cards. It was late when Nurse Winthrop pushed open the door to Mrs. Demming's bedroom. "All right you kids. Out! Mrs. Demming has had a very long day and needs her rest!"

"Can't we stay just a while longer?" Madison pleaded. "After all, it is Christmas Eve!"

"Sorry. Rules are rules and we must keep to her medicinal time schedule. Now out! Here you are Mrs. Demming. Here's a nice warm glass of milk that will help you sleep tonight! You want to be bright and chipper for Christmas tomorrow, don't you?"

"Yes, I most certainly do." Mrs. Demming took the glass from Nurse Winthrop and put it to her lips. She saw the horror in Madison's eyes, but winked to reassure her that she had no intention of drinking it. When Nurse Winthrop turned to hustle the kids out of the room, she quickly poured the contents into the plant that stood on her night stand.

"Goodnight, Mom!" Madison called from the door.

"Goodnight, Maddie!"

"There! Now wasn't that good?" Nurse Winthrop took the empty glass with a smile. She pulled up the blankets, walked away, then turned at the door, "Goodnight, Mrs. Demming. Pleasant dreams!" She turned out the lights and left.

They had agreed to leave the lights off and for an hour Madison paced back and forth in her darkened room. Kurt and Willie were staring out the window. A snowflake floated here and there and dark clouds rolled in obscuring the moon. In seconds the single flake had multiplied to millions. Zola sat in a chair near the door which was left ajar just enough for her to keep an eye on the hall.

"See him?" Kurt whispered to Willie and pointed. "He's on his way."

"Great, Zola, someone coming in the back. Keep a sharp eye!" Willie called out to her.

"Did you see who it was?" Madison rushed over to the window.

"No, just a shadow, keep quiet. He should be coming through any minute." They all tip-toed to the door and stood with Zola. They all held their breath, waited a few moments, then closed the door, ears pressed against it.

Several minutes later a shadow appeared in the hall, closing the door very quietly to the unoccupied wing . The intruder crept along the wall keeping beneath the hall lights until he was standing in front of Mrs. Demming's door. With a look to his left and to his right, he very quietly twisted the door handle and stepped inside, just as slowly and quietly closing the door behind him.

The figure walked up to the bed and stared down at the sleeping face of Rozlin Demming. For several long minutes he stared, his hands, gloved in dark leather, twisting and flexing until he finally decided it was time. He gave her a gentle shake and stepped back. Rozlin opened her eyes and gasped in horror. "Tonight you will die! Tonight you will wander into the snow storm and they will not find you until you are dead. Dead and gone!" She bolted upright, pulling the blankets to her throat.

"Not tonight!" She screamed and reached for the lamp on her nightstand. She flicked on the lamp and stared in horror as the figure came to life in the glare of the lamp.

"You....you're supposed to be drugged! You're supposed to..." the hooded figure cried.

"Collin!" Rozlin cried when she recognized the voice. "But...but...why?"

"Why? You dare ask why?" Collin Demming tore the covering from his face. There was no point in hiding any longer. "All these years I've put up with you. Put up with that tight wad old man penny pinching his millions, tossing me scraps like I was some stupid mongrel dog at the end of his leash! I ran up such debt, you see. I needed money and when I went to him he laughed in my face. Told me what a

[211]

disappointment I was. Not even man enough to sire a son. So I obliged. I had a son. Then the old fool tugs my chains again. Instead of giving me the money I wanted, he changed his will and left it all to Madison and Zane. What a fool I was!"

"But Collin! Madison and Zane are your children! Your flesh and blood!" Rozlin cried.

"Flesh and blood! What is that compared to the millions that old man promised! No one ever thought his death had been other than natural. We frightened him with ghostly apparitions until he suffered his heart attack, shut off the air in his tank and waited for him to stop breathing. It was so simple. And then what? Then I find he left you, *you* as legal trustee of the money for Madison and Zane. What else could I do, Roz, dear?"

"You....you have done all this for the money? Why? Why?"

"Greed." Collin Demming shrugged his shoulders nonchalantly. "What other motive could there be? After tonight you'll be dead, found frozen somewhere in the snow, having been depressed over this Christmas holiday that you just couldn't tolerate even just one more day."

"You would ruin Madison's Christmas!"

"Oh, my dear Roz, Madison will be so heart-broken that she will have taken one too many sleeping pills. And Zane? Well I won't have to worry about Zane for some time, will I? By that time, everyone will have forgotten about how you and Madison died and the money will all be mine!"

The door of the bedroom flew open and Madison turned on the overhead lights. "Dad? Dad how could you?" Collin Demming spun around.

"Oh, Maddie, Maddie! Why did you have to go and do that for? You've just ruined everything," Collin Demming sneered at her. Madison stared unbelieving at the man before her. His face was so distorted by greed and hate she hardly recognized him. She gave a sharp cry and stepped back.

"No, you don't my dear," Collin Demming said reaching for her. "You have left me no choice but to take care of both you and your mother tonight."

"I think not," Sheriff Brandon stepped out from the sitting room, his weapon drawn. Deputy Calhoun followed in from the hall and quickly put cuffs on Collin Demming. Zola gripped Madison's hand and dragged her out of the way.

"You'll have a tough time proving anything, Sheriff. After all, I can say I was here to visit my sick and deranged wife for the holidays. You have nothing!" Collin Demming shouted.

"I think we do," Sheriff Brandon said. "Barb?"

Barbara McLeish came out of the bathroom carrying a tape recorder. She played back the last few lines and Collin Demming's face turned ashen.

"It wasn't all my idea!" he shouted. "It wasn't all me! Reuben Delasky was the one who suggested this! He set up the whole haunting thing with that nurse!"

"We know." Kurt said when he and Willie arrived at the door and shoved Nurse Winthrop inside. "Caught her trying to sneak down the hall, Dad! Great job, by the way, Madison."

"Good work boys. Let's take care of these two, Cliff, and get a warrant out for the arrest of Reuben Delasky before he can flee the country. Come on you two."

Cliff quickly put a set of cuffs on Nurse Winthrop and was ushering them out the door. Madison jumped on the bed, hugging her mom. Barbara McLeish sat on the edge of the bed and grasped Rozlin's hand and gave it a squeeze.

"Dad! I almost forgot!" Kurt shouted. "Mom called. She's at the hospital!"

"What!" Robert Brandon cried.

"I couldn't tell you earlier and ruin the set up. She called a long time ago."

"Go! Go!" Cliff Calhoun shouted to him. "I've got additional back up on the way!"

"Thanks, Cliff. Come on Kurt!" Brandon started for the stairs. Kurt ran to catch up. He turned abruptly and ran back to the bedroom.

"Well?" he shouted at Willie. "You coming?"

Margaret Brandon sat propped up in the bed, a tiny pink blanket curled in her arms. "You boys sure took your sweet time!" she smiled at them.

Robert Brandon bent to kiss his wife then gently touched the pink blanket. Kurt stared down at the tiny face, with its pink cheeks and dark blue eyes staring back.

"Oh, Mom!" he touched the soft down of gold hair that covered the top of her head and reached for the tiny fingers that opened and closed near her face. The tiny fingers touched his and wrapped around holding tight. "Wow what a grip! She's so beautiful! She's so perfect! Mom!"

"I know," Kurt's mom beamed at him. "What a perfect Christmas gift! So what have you thought of for a name?"

"I was thinking of Kate, or Kathleen, something like that," Robert Brandon said.

"No, she's definitely not a Kate or a Kathleen, Dad, that's too girlie, she's got a grip like a wrestler! I was thinking that because she's a Christmas baby why don't we name her Christa, or Christi you know....for Christmas? Maybe something like Christa Jane?"

"What a lovely name!" Margaret smiled. "Christa Jane. What do you think, Rob?"

"I think it's beautiful!"

"Really? You both like it?" Kurt exclaimed.

"We love it. Christa Jane. That's her name."

"Well, well, well, little C.J.," Kurt wiggled the little fist still clenched tight to his finger.

"Oh dear, starting that already?" Kurt's mom laughed.

Willie nudged Kurt in the ribs. "Oh yeah, Dad, Willie and I have a favor to ask. We need a ride to Old Brunswicktown."

"I don't think there's going to be any stores open today, son," Rob Brandon said. "Especially not now, it's one in the morning."

"No, it's not at a store. It's from a private person. We have to pick up the gift for Mrs. Hendicott. Can you give us a ride?"

"Of course, first thing in the morning. We'll go to early services first. Well, my dear. We'd better leave you to feed our little Christa Jane. I suppose this means we celebrate Christmas a little late this year."

"Who cares! It's been a great day so far, right Dad?" Kurt beamed and pried his finger from the tight grip. "Come on. We'd better get going."

The following day sped by, first church, then a quick trip to Old Brunswicktown and the afternoon at the hospital. Kurt and his father decided to hold off opening their gifts until Margie and Christa Jane could join them. They joined Willie and his parents for supper and finally the boys were able to get away.

"You going back to the hospital, Dad?" Kurt asked zipping up his jacket.

"Yes, one last visit for the night."

"We'll see you there, okay Dad? We have to see Mrs. Hendicott first."

"Just go straight home, son. Visiting hours will be over soon and I'm sure your mother needs her rest."

"Okay, tell her........." Kurt looked around somewhat embarrassed in front of everyone.... "tell you...well, you know!" He hurried out the door with Willie.

"Do you think she'll like it?" he asked Willie when they were out of sight.

"You know she's going to love it!" Willie grinned.

They entered the porch which was brightly decorated with strings of Christmas lights. After removing boots and jackets, they set their surprise gift for Mrs. Hendicott in the hall.

"In the parlor, boys!" Mrs. Hendicott called out merrily. "I was so excited to hear about your little Christmas bundle, Kurt. What a lovely surprise!"

"I know. Mom is so happy!" Kurt exclaimed.

"Sit, sit. I have a surprise gift for each of you." Mrs. Hendicott rose to retrieve two small Christmas wrapped gifts from beneath the table tree that decorated the corner of the parlor. "I found these while going through some of Horace's things and thought you might like them. Go ahead! Open them!" She rubbed her hands together excitedly.

The boys tore the wrappings off and whistled. The small ebony carved boxes were brightly polished and had a glass cover on the top. "Spanish Gold Escudo, Lima Peru, 1709," Kurt read the engraved inscription. "Wow! Are these real?"

"As real as anything else my grandfather pilfered as a pirate."

"Wow! These are great, Mrs. Hendicott!" Kurt exclaimed. "Thanks!"

"Yeah, thanks!" Willie echoed. "Hey, we have something for you, too."

"Oh my, you boys didn't have to get me anything," Mrs. Hendicott began but Kurt cut her off.

"Course we didn't *have to* but we *wanted to* so hurry and go get it Willie!"

Willie went to retrieve the basket, it's large red bow draped down the sides. He returned and set it in Mrs. Hendicott's lap.

"What is this? A picnic basket?" She looked at them questioningly.

"Open it. You have to open it!" Kurt grinned. He elbowed Willie.

"Beautiful bow," Mrs. Hendicott untied it then lifted the basket up and down. "Too light to have a picnic lunch in it, I suppose."

"Open it!" both boys cried together.

Mrs. Hendicott lifted the lid. A sharp intake of breath and tears welled in her eyes. Nestled on a pink blanket covered in black kitty paws prints was a tiny calico kitten that was yawning and stretching as it awoke from its slumber. "She's exactly like Missy!" Kurt cried. "Same markings and everything!"

Mrs. Hendicott picked up the tiny kitten and buried her face in its soft fur. "She's so beautiful!"

"Happy Christmas, Mrs. Hendicott!" Kurt and Willie cried together, the tiny scars on their thumbs meeting once more.